A Wish Upon the Wind

We hope you enjoy this special Christmas story, written by the brother of one of our dear Oneida friends, Cathy Cornue. Cathy's husband, Don, designed the cover... and, the ornament is a true Pittman family tradition. May all of your Family Traditions be memorable for you and all of yours! M&L 2008

Merry Christmas, 2008
Cheryl & Tim -

Peace & Love —
Maggie & Lenny

Also by Joseph Pittman

Fiction:

Tilting at Windmills

When the World Was Small

Legend's End

Mystery:

London Frog: A Todd Gleason Crime Novel

California Scheming: A Todd Gleason Crime Novel (forthcoming)

A WISH UPON THE WIND

A Linden Corners Christmas

JOSEPH PITTMAN

iUniverse, Inc.
New York Bloomington

A Wish Upon the Wind
A Linden Corners Christmas

iUniverse books may be ordered through booksellers or by contacting:

iUniverse
1663 Liberty Drive
Bloomington, IN 47403
www.iuniverse.com
1-800-Authors (1-800-288-4677)

ISBN: 978-0-595-53520-0 (pbk)
ISBN: 978-0-595-63581-8 (ebk)

Printed in the United States of America

iUniverse rev. date: 10/21/08

This one's for…

Pittman Christmas

Mom & Dad

Cathy & Don, Jerry & Louise, Liz & Doug, Larry & Terri,
Michael, Peggy & Jeff

Jon & Cindi and Xavier, David & Milena, Brian, Ben & Amanda,
Nate, Josh, Jerry, Christopher, Dan & Lisa, Stephanie, Eric, Kevin, Libby, P.J., Michelle, Jessica, Michael, Anthony, Sarah, Jen and Andrew.

We sure fill a room, don't we?

"Let it be said that of all who give gifts,
these two were the wisest."

—O. Henry, "The Gift of the Maji"

You've been here before, this place called Linden Corners. There was once the tale of a man, a woman, a young girl, a windmill…and a terrible storm that forever changed their lives. Many of you wondered what happened next. If you are new to the inspiring, enduring tale of the windmill, you need no prior knowledge, this story stands alone.

You are all cordially invited to celebrate the holidays with Brian, Janey, and the rest of the Linden Corners family.

Turn the page, there are gifts waiting to be unwrapped…

PROLOGUE

Theirs was a seemingly unbreakable bond, one that had been built by the power of the wind and by the presence of the mighty windmill. Today, the sails of that windmill spun its special brand of magic, even as the harshness of winter approached and nature readied to hibernate for the long, cold months ahead.

On this Wednesday afternoon in November, he found himself walking through the light coating of snow that covered the ground, venturing to the base of the windmill. It was here, on this eve of the holiday season, he sought inspiration and knowledge and strength, all of which he would need to delicately negotiate his way through the memories of a past that threatened to undo their fragile happiness. Because as wonderful as they were together, life hadn't always been easy, and the coming month would prove to be the most trying time yet, a test of that bond.

"Annie, can you hear me?" he asked aloud, hoping the wind would carry his words forward, upward. "Because I

need your help, Janey needs your help, and I know you're the only one who can show me—show us—the way through. Thanksgiving is coming, Annie, and how I wish you were here to celebrate with us, it would have been our first. Before long Christmas will be upon us, and if we can get through that, I think we'll be fine, just fine. Until then, Annie, I just can't predict how Janey will react to certain situations. Can you help me, can you show me the way to make this holiday a special one for your daughter? She's eight and she's alone except for me and sometimes I wonder, Annie, am I enough for her?"

There was no answer, not today. Snowflakes fell lightly, the wind was gentle and the sails spun slowly, as though the windmill itself could anticipate the quiet soon to descend on the tiny village of Linden Corners, on its residents and on its way of life. For Brian Duncan, this coming season would be a growing experience, knowing the success of the holidays rested solely on his shoulders. And as much as he looked forward to it, there were times when his heart was frozen with fear, when uncertainty stopped him in his step. Now, as they prepared to briefly journey beyond Linden Corners, panic once again seized him, a feeling he usually sensed only after Janey had gone to sleep, when the night awakened his insecurities. Often he went to Annie for assistance, and standing now in the shadow of the windmill, he began to realize she couldn't always be there for him. Some decisions he had to make on his own.

"I told my mother, Annie, that I wasn't coming for Thanksgiving unless she made peach pie," Brian said with a touch of levity he thought was needed. He had been introduced to the sweet pie just this past summer on a picnic high above the lazy river, on a rocky ridge he named for her. Annie's Bluff. "She claimed never to have heard of such a pie. I had to search your recipe box, and even after I found it I doubted it would taste the same. A piece of pie for Janey, knowing it's a piece of you."

Still there came no answer, just gentle wind and falling flakes and the languid spin of the sails, nothing different, no sign. Just then Brian smiled, perhaps interpreting this silence as an acknowledgment—that if the wind didn't see fit to change, neither should he. Steady the course, and follow your instincts, follow your heart.

"Okay, Annie, I think I hear you now," he said.

He placed his hand on the windmill's door, as though seeking a pulse. Then, turning back toward the farmhouse, he saw Janey emerging from over the hill, her fingers laced through those of Gerta Connors, neighbor and friend, honorary grandmother. They both waved at him, and Janey broke free and began to run down the hill, her boots making faint impressions on the snow, like she was barely touching the ground.

"Brian, Brian, I'm ready, let's go. We've got a long drive ahead of us," she said with easy glee, conjured from

her redoubtable spirit. Then she wrapped herself around his waist and held him tight.

"I was just making sure everything was secure," he said. "I see now that it is."

Together, they made their way back up the hill where Gerta waited. Gerta, who had invited them to spend Thanksgiving with her and her four grown daughters, Gerta who had herself faced loss this past year and persevered, just like them all. Brian had politely declined her offer; maybe they both needed this first holiday with their own families, he explained. Holidays are about families, she should be with hers and he, his.

"My mother, she needs her family most during these times," Brian stated. "A time when the Duncan family remembers what we have, what we lost. Maybe the only time we do remember."

In every family there were both treasures lost and found, traditions to be upheld. Gerta had understood.

Back at the farmhouse, Brian and Janey said their good-byes to Gerta, and then piled into Brian's car, suitcases already in the trunk.

"Ready?" Brian asked Janey.

"I already said so," she replied, not without a sense of exasperation that reminded him of Annie. Of the time they had first met, here, at the windmill.

Soon they were on the road out of Linden Corners, passing the windmill as they did so. Janey waved to it, and Brian, smiling nonetheless, he just kept driving. Because he'd already made his wish upon the wind, and it was up to nature now to send his message to that special place where all wishes belonged.

PART ONE

Old Traditions

CHAPTER ONE

If tradition dictates the direction of your life, it was inevitable then that my mother would call me two weeks before Thanksgiving to ask whether I would be joining the family for dinner. Every year she makes the same call, every year she asks in her unassuming way, and every year I respond in my expected fashion. Yes, of course, where else would I be? This year, though, so much had changed—in my life and in my parents' too—that I had to wonder whether the notion of tradition belonged to a bygone era, appreciated only by thoughts of the past. How I answered my mother on this day proved that indeed change was in the air. Because I informed her that before I could give her an answer, I needed to consult first with Janey.

"Brian, dear, you don't ask children what they want to do, you tell them," she stated.

"No, mother, Janey and I, we're a team. We make decisions together."

Before hanging up I was told that I had much to learn about raising children, which left me brooding the remainder of the day, even when Janey came home from school filled with a light that usually brightened me. I waited, though, until bedtime to ask Janey her thoughts on the subject.

"Thanksgiving? Away from Linden Corners?"

I nodded. "It's your call."

"Do you want to go, Brian?"

"I will if you will," I replied.

"Then I will if you will," she said, her smile uplifting.

As night fell and she slept, I phoned my mother back and told her to add two plates to the dinner table, the Linden Corners faction of the family would join them.

"You know how much this means to me, Brian."

Yes, I did.

And while accepting the invitation may have been a relatively smooth process at the time, now, as we turned the corner off Walnut Street in Philadelphia and were only two blocks from my parents' new home, anxiety and trepidation ran through me like Montezuma's revenge. The trip had taken us six hours (with a dinner break), but really, it had been an even longer time coming. Nine months had passed since I'd last seen my parents, and in that elapsed time my world had drastically changed in a way none of us could have predicted. I had quit my well-paying job as a corporate drone, sublet my tiny New York apartment, and left behind the supposed woman of my dreams, setting out on a journey that would take me not far from all I'd known in terms of miles, yet worlds away. I'd met Annie Sullivan and I'd loved her and I'd lost her, and as a result had been given the care of her daughter, eight-year-old Janey Sullivan, a wonder of a girl, the true girl of my dreams. Since then, I hadn't allowed any visitors, whether friends or family, to stay with us, wanting this time of transition between me and Janey to take shape without any further disruptions. Even now I had my concerns about taking this precious girl out from the safe confines of her life, but realized too there was a time for everything, even for moving forward.

"Which house is it?" Janey asked, pointing out the car window at the long row of houses lining both sides of the dimly-lit street. This was Society Hill, where Federal-style townhouses prevailed, these classic, restored buildings adorning each side of the street, their facades brick covered and trimmed in white. I didn't blame Janey for being confused, they all looked the same. Still, I indicated the building on the far left-hand corner. "With the porch light on."

"Good thing, since it's so dark. How else would we find it?"

"Well, Janey, I do have the address."

"Oh," she replied with a giggle that made me grin. That was a good thing right now.

I found parking on a side street, left the suitcases behind for now, and with Janey's hand in mine, made my way toward the upscale house of Kevin and Didi Duncan. For years they had lived in the Philly suburbs (in the house I'd grown up in) and had just this past summer done the opposite of all their friends, they had gone urban, selling the old house and instead buying this very nice home in this very nice section of the city of Brotherly Love. I had yet to see it for myself, thinking this was a good thing, there were no memories of past holidays awaiting me behind those doors. Though you can never really escape memories no matter the walls you've built up, your mind could tear them down whenever it chose. As we reached the steps, I looked down at Janey's freckled face and asked, "Ready?"

"You keep asking that," she said. "I think the question is, are you ready?"

"And I think the answer is: Not really."

"Silly, Brian—they're your parents."

Exactly.

Then, as if Janey's words were a magic key, the front door opened and a bath of light from inside illuminated us, sending our shadows retreating to the sidewalk. Yet we stepped forward to where my mother waited in the entranceway. She was dressed in a simple navy skirt and white silk blouse, a string of pearls dangling from her neck. Her graying hair was salon perfect; she wouldn't be Didi Duncan if not properly attired, even at this hour.

"Well, who have we here?" she asked.

"Your son," I replied dryly, and then Janey said, "And me, I'm Janey."

My mother moved off the top step and gave me a fast embrace before bending down so her face was level with Janey's. "Well, you're a pretty young thing, aren't you, Jane?"

"Janey," I corrected her.

"That's such a childish name, now, don't you think?"

"I am a child," Janey remarked.

"Nonsense, dear. You've had to grow tremendously the last few months, haven't you? Come in, come in the both of you."

And we did, shutting out the encroaching cold behind us. We entered a hallway crafted lovingly with antique wood, and then were ushered down to the living room where a warm fire was blazing in the fireplace. My father, Kevin Duncan, sat beside the fire in a wingback chair, still dressed in his business suit, the tie still on, the top button to his shirt still clasped. He was reading the *Wall Street Journal* and on the table near him was a tasteful glass of cognac, the successful entrepreneur in relaxation mode. When he saw us enter, he gently set the paper down on a nearby ottoman.

"Hello, son, it's good to see you," he said, shaking my hand with his strong, firm grip. His greeting was as efficient and business-like as ever; it was just his way, all his world had taught him. He was a tall man, six four and built strongly, and I imagined in his office, even if he hadn't been the boss he would still strike an intimidating pose. Yet a surprising feat happened on this evening. As Janey poked out from behind me, she craned her neck up high so she could see my father and that's when she exclaimed, "Wow, you're big," a surprise because that businessman's face crumbled and a smile found its way to his stern face.

"Well, let's get a good look at you, young lady," he said.

"You'd have to sit on the floor to do that."

Kevin Duncan, thinning gray hair and bespeckled, a big barrel of a man, actually laughed, something he didn't actually list on his resume. Then, instead of doing as Janey suggested, he lifted the little girl into those big arms of his and I realized that the impossible had been accomplished, Janey had softened the heart of a big-moneyed giant. I felt tension leave my shoulders and I realized then that maybe this Thanksgiving holiday wouldn't be so bad. The four of us settled into the living room and talked, Janey having a glass of juice and me a seltzer, while my father and mother drank their cognac, their attention focused mostly on Janey. They asked her questions about school and friends, nothing about her mother Annie or the difficult times this girl had already known in her life. As they chatted, I sat on the edge of my seat, waiting anxiously for any misstep.

About ten o'clock, the excitement of the trip and of Janey meeting my parents finally over, I retrieved the suitcases from the car and attempted to get Janey settled into her guest room. She was busy looking at the old photographs my parents had hung on the walls.

"Is that you, Brian?" Janey asked, pointing to a geeky teen posing for his high school graduation picture. When I told her it was, she laughed. "You look different now—better." As I thanked her, she pointed to the other two portraits that hung above mine, one of a dark-haired young man, the other a young woman. Again, high graduation pictures. "Who are they?"

"That's Rebecca; she's my sister."

"She's pretty. And who's the other guy? He doesn't look so..."

"Geeky?"

"Yeah," she said, with an impish smile.

Before answering her question, I myself stared at the photograph up for discussion, thought of the memories his classically handsome face inspired. For a second I looked around for the trophies and awards, and then remembered this was no longer his room, it wasn't even the house he'd grown up in. Any of us, actually. I wondered how my parents had felt packing up the old house, saying good-bye to a room that had for years remained fixed in time. Then I answered.

"That's my brother. His name was Philip."

Our conversation was interrupted as my mother came brushing through the doorway. When she saw what little progress I'd made in getting Janey to sleep, she tossed me out.

"What do you know about little girls, Brian?"

My mother liked to ask questions, but she seldom waited for answers. Tonight was no different. Truth be known, I could have answered her with easy confidence because I knew a lot, Janey had helped me plenty since I'd become her legal guardian. But for now I let my mother enjoy fussing over Janey, said my goodnights and retreated to the other guest room. And as I fought to find sleep that night, I hoped that tomorrow and in the coming weeks, I would be able to reciprocate with Janey, because I had a feeling that special little girl was going to need all the help she could get.

* * *

We would be eight people for a four o'clock dinner, and so Janey and I spent a good portion of the morning touring the nearby historic district of Philadelphia, even though most of the sites were closed down for the holiday. Still, it gave us an opportunity to escape the house while preparations were made and so when we returned at just after one the table was set with my grandmother's fine china and crystal, yet another Duncan family tradition. Also, the first guests had arrived, my parents' best friends and my father's business partner, Harry Henderson and his (third) wife, Katrina, both of whom sat in the living room with glasses of white wine and nibbling on imported cheese and crackers. Both Hendersons were impeccably dressed. Both Janey and I changed into more suitable clothes for my mother's formal Thanksgiving, returning downstairs for proper introductions. I had met the Hendersons on numerous occasions, so this time it was Janey in the spotlight. As she politely smiled at them, I wondered how much they'd been briefed on Janey's situation—and found out sooner than I had wanted.

"You're very pretty," Harry said.

"Yes, it's very nice to meet you, Janey," Katrina Henderson said. "I bet Brian's just the best Dad. You're very lucky."

A silence descended on the room, the crackling of the fire the only audible sound. My father looked at me with apology and my mother put a hand to her mouth, trying in vain to keep the sharp "eek" from coming out. It was Janey, though, who took control of the situation, when she simply and innocently said, "Oh, Brian's not my Dad. He's...he's Brian, and he takes very good care of me."

"Of course he does, dear," my mother said, coming up behind Janey, nearly forcing her from the room with the promise of a sweet treat, as though that action could remove the awkwardness that settled over the room.

"I'm so sorry, Brian, I didn't know what to refer to you as," Katrina said, "and, well, you must admit, it's an uncomfortable situation to be placed in."

"I'm glad you think so, imagine how Janey feels. Excuse me," I said, and went after her.

I found her sitting at the kitchen table drinking a glass of apple juice while my mother basted the turkey; and here I thought she was comforting Janey, not just attending to the bird. I asked my mother if I could have a moment alone with Janey, and thankfully the ringing of the doorbell saved me from having to ask twice. She tossed down a dishtowel and asked that I take over at the oven, "the turkey needs attention."

Well, so did Janey.

"You okay?" I asked.

She nodded while taking a prolonged sip from the glass.

"You say the word, we can go home, probably be home in time to..."

"To sleep," she said. "It's a long drive, remember?"

"We'll leave tomorrow morning, okay?"

She set the glass down, scrunching her nose at me. "Brian, what's a tradition?"

"It's...well, it's when you do the same thing all the time," I said, knowing that wasn't the best definition I could come up with. "Okay, here's an example. You know how I explained that I have always had Thanksgiving dinner with my parents? That's a tradition. And at Christmas time, we always decorate the tree the night before, just in time for Santa to come and bring presents. It's the way we've done it year after year, from even before my parents had any children. I think that's how it worked when they were kids, too."

"Wow, Christmas Eve? That's really late for putting up the tree. Mom and I, we always chop our own tree down and set it up long before Christmas, like two weeks ahead."

"See, that's a tradition, Janey. It's your tradition."

"Oh," she said. She smiled widely as she realized that even she, at the young age of eight, had her share of traditions.

Her mood brightened and the awkwardness from before dissipated, and we rejoined the party in the living room. The last two guests had arrived. My sister, Rebecca Louise Duncan Samson Herbert, and her latest boyfriend, who I learned was named Rex, probably the first Rex I'd ever met, would probably be the last. Rebecca was ten years my senior and Rex was ten years her junior and said "nice to meet you, dude." Rebecca was twice divorced and turned out Rex never married, so the two of them were seemingly a perfect fit. My sister kissed my cheek, Rex shook my hand ghetto-style, and they both waved unenthusiastically when introduced to Janey.

"Where's Junior?" I asked my sister.

"With his father, the bastard," she said, though it wasn't clear who was the bastard, the ex or her son. With my sister, you just never know. Then, when she noticed Janey still clinging to my side, she apologized for her language. "Oops, sorry, not used to kids being around."

This from a mother.

Junior was her son by her first husband, he was ten-years-old and would have been a nice playmate today (I had expected my sister to bring her son, not some dim-witted boy-toy), because I realized Janey was lost amidst this churning sea of adults. What did she have in common with this group of people? Heck, what did I? Rebecca went off in search of a drink, Rex followed her, ever the dutiful puppy, and when no one else was looking, Janey turned back to me and said, "Could we go and look at the Liberty Bell again?"

"It wasn't open the first time, Janey."

"I know," she replied, which had me stifling a laugh.

No one heard the exchange, busy with their own small talk.

We were both a far cry from the gentle comfort of Linden Corners, and we found that our homey farmhouse was calling to us. I imagined Gerta sitting down to a table filled with food and love, her four daughters and sons-in-law, their sweet children, the kind of Thanksgiving you saw perfected on Hallmark television. What gave those assembled here the illusion of perfection was the table, which overflowed with food, a huge turkey that my father delighted in carving, "like a takeover, removing it piece by piece," he said, getting a hearty laugh out of that sycophant Harry. There were also potatoes and dressing and cranberries and rolls and warm crusty breads, vegetables too, a feast to satisfy ourselves on. Good thing, too, the conversation might have starved us.

My father and Harry talked business—stocks and the ups and down of the economy—and my mother and Katrina talked about society concerns, only to be interrupted by Rebecca, who was reminding us of how she met Rex. She decided then we needed to know all the details, relating the story of a society function for a local hospital that was "dull, dull, dull, really, I could have died, except for the fact that I met good ol' Rexy."

Janey giggled. "Finally, someone else whose name sounds good when you add a 'y' at the end. That's how Brian and I met—at the windmill, where I called him Brian-y and then said yuck. That doesn't sound good, does it?"

"Not in the least," said my mother.

"What's this about a windmill?" Katrina asked.

"It was my mom's," Janey said. "It's really big, and it's beautiful, and Brian likes it too, don't you, Brian? It has giant sails and sometimes I imagine it spins stories, and I go there to hear them, because it's really my mom telling them to me."

Janey's flurry of words quieted the table, and it was my father who broke the silence when he looked at her with sudden pride and said, "You must have inherited your mother's trait for telling stories, because I liked that one very much. Thank you, Janey, for gracing our Thanksgiving table with your sweet presence."

"You're welcome," she said. "Thank you for inviting me."

"Anytime, Jane," my mother said. "You are just delightful."

Both of my parents caught my eye, and I mouthed a quick "thank you," even forgiving my mother her petty quirk of calling Janey "Jane."

"Oh, Brian," Rebecca said, taking command of the table again, "I meant to tell you the moment I saw you, I also ran into Lucy Watkins at that charity event. She said to say 'hello.'"

"Who's Lucy?" Janey asked.

"No one," I said, dismissively.

"Lucy was Brian's first love—oh, they dated all through high school and college and it seemed like one day they would have the most wonderful wedding," my mother said. Leave it my mother to think about the wedding day and not what was to follow. "I hear she has two children and that her husband is a doctor. She's done quite well for herself, Lucy has."

Janey tossed me an odd look that I couldn't read, and then whatever she was thinking she dropped it. I easily let it go, allowing the remainder of dinner to pass uneventfully. All of us had our fill of food and drink, all of us were thankful for what we had, this feast and the company that enveloped us and the prosperity that surrounded us.

As the empty plates were cleared and dessert dishes were set at each place setting, my mother announced that this was the time for us all to say what we were most thankful for. I had been hoping to spare Janey this ritual, thinking it might be a struggle for this girl who had lost so much this year to find something to be thankful for.

"I thought we were beyond doing this kind of thing," I said.

"Brian, it's a Duncan family tradition, you know that—albeit slightly altered over the years." And she proceeded to tell how this particular event had once upon a time preceded the meal, "until Kevin's repeated complaints about the turkey getting cold made us move it to dessert time. We used to have such large dinners, so many people sitting amongst us during a time there was so much to be thankful for." My mother lost her train of thought and I sensed she was remembering Philip, which always left her flustered. She managed to recover by saying, "Rebecca always had so much to be thankful for, didn't you dear?"

"I'll be short and sweet tonight," Rebecca offered.

"I'm always thankful for dessert," Janey said.

"Good," my mother said, "Jane got us off to a marvelous start. Anyone else?"

As we went around the table, I kept a careful eye on Janey, wondering if she had said all she wished to, and after my Dad got his turn, glad his fortunes had prevailed in the marketplace this year, and Mom, thrilled with her new house, Rebecca and Rex thankful for finding each other, the Henderson's each with their own shallow thanks, all eyes turned to me.

I was ready, I'd thought about it. "I'm thankful for the power of the wind, which blows through our lives and changes its direction on a whim, grateful that it landed me in Linden Corners and at the base of that unexpected windmill. I'm thankful for the time I shared with Annie Sullivan, and mostly I'm thankful for her beautiful daughter, Janey, who even when the sun doesn't come up lights up my life."

"That was very nice, Brian, very, uh...heartfelt," my mother stated. "Now, who wants pie? I've got apple, pumpkin, even a peach pie—at Brian's request...oh, yes, Jane, what is it?"

Janey had interrupted my mother by raising her hand. "Don't I get a turn, you know, to say what I'm thankful for?"

"You did, dear, you were thankful for dessert. So, peach pie, is it?"

"Mom, let her speak."

The room again quieted down as Janey found all eyes descended on her. She focused her own eyes at me, uncertainty suddenly written in them. I gave her my hand as a gesture of support, which she gratefully accepted. "I shouldn't really have any reason to be thankful, not this year. Awful things happened, terrible things that took from me the person I most loved, the only person I thought I could depend on. But maybe that was selfish thinking, because I know now that I'm really lucky, because I've got Brian, and even if he's not my real father, well, he's someone very special. He's my best friend, and I'm thankful that I get to share his..." She paused, looking at me, watching tears fall from my eyes as she smiled and said, "Share his traditions and his family."

A new tradition began that day. A kinder, warmer Duncan Thanksgiving was born, the child among us teaching us a lesson we'd not soon forget.

* * *

Janey was long asleep as eleven o'clock rolled around, and I too was ready to turn in. We were planning to leave first thing in the morning. Though my place of employ, George's Tavern, had been closed for the holiday, the weekend was our busy time and I needed to be there. Yet there remained one more act of the show that was a Duncan's celebration, and I found my parents asking me into the living room.

"We wanted to talk with you—a serious conversation, dear," my mother said, exchanging glances with my looming father. "Brian, I have to confess, when you first told us what had happened up there in that town, about that poor woman..."

"Annie, who I planned to marry."

"Yes, Annie," she said, as though she knew her, had met her and come to love her. "We were worried about, uh, Annie…having left the care of her daughter in your hands. After all, Brian, you became a city kid, a New Yorker. You know about take-out meals and late-nights out with your friends. What could you possibly know about raising kids? That's what we thought. But seeing you with Jane today, how remarkable the two of you are together, I suppose we don't have to worry so much. I know I don't express my emotions very easily, I'm the first to admit that, but you're very good with Jane. You are very patient and understanding."

"You listen to her," my father interjected. "That's important."

"Thank you, that means a lot," I said.

"Yes, well, that only makes what we're about to tell you a bit easier," she said. "I know tradition is an important thing for you, which is why it was important you were here today. Believe us, Brian, we appreciate your effort; so does Rebecca. We all remember...the family we once were. We also recognize that Jane must have her own way of doing things, and since Christmas is coming up..."

"What your mother is attempting to say, Brian, is this: we're suddenly faced with the idea of having our first Christmas away from our children—we assume you'll be busy with Janey. And Rebecca, well, who knows what crazy act she'll come up with this year. So, rather than spend a quiet and, ugh, remorseful holiday, we've decided not to be home for Christmas this year. We've scheduled a Caribbean cruise with the Hendersons. And though we were nervous about changing things up this year, I think maybe it's been a good decision. Now Janey can enjoy the holiday in her own home, with no pressure for you to join us. We hope you're okay with this."

I had said nothing during this exchange, letting them both speak their minds, prepared for the worst but comforted and soothed by their words. A bit surprised, too. All day long I had worried that my parents had become fixated on the less important parts of life, their money and their home, forgetting the wonderful things in life that you *could* take with you. Though no doubt they would spoil themselves rotten on their upcoming cruise, the idea behind it, the selflessness surrounding their gesture warmed me. I found myself embracing them both, a scene as unlikely as any you'd find inside these historic walls.

Two more gifts awaited me, one I took with pleasure, the other with great reluctance. My mother had dug through the boxes of Christmas decorations and handed me a box and inside it was a shiny blue ball, my name written across it in silver lettering. When I held it in my hands, a lump lodged in my throat. I had briefly forgotten about it and now felt guilty.

"Thank you, thank you for remembering to give this to me," I said. "It means...a lot."

Nothing further needed to be said about it. Everyone in the family had one of these name balls, and every year I had hung mine on my parents' tree.

"This year, Brian, hang it on your own tree," my mother said.

Afterward, sniffling slightly, she excused herself, leaving me alone with my father. He resumed his role as unflappable businessman as he proceeded to hand me a thin envelope. "Raising a child is an expensive proposition, Brian, and last I knew you didn't really have a job. Oh, I know, you've got that tavern, but that's not enough, can't be near enough. Probably your savings are shaved down to the bone. And before you refuse our help out of some sense of pride or whatever, think about what matters most. Think of who this money will benefit most."

I didn't protest, just slipped the envelope into my pocket without looking at it. Our meeting was over, and I went to bed, checking first on Janey, who was fast asleep. Only when I was behind closed doors did I open the envelope and look at the check my father had presented me with. I slept fitfully that night.

When we said good-bye the next morning my father swung Janey around in his arms until she was laughing uncontrollably, my mother then pecking her cheek, saying, "Good-bye, Janey."

Such progress.

And despite the check for $25,000 from my father, I think the richness of the holiday was left behind inside that gilded townhouse.

As we both piled into the car, I gently set on the backseat the precious box which contained my family Christmas ornament. Janey grew curious about it and so I told her she could take it out of the box, but carefully.

"Oh, wow, Brian, it's so pretty," she said, her eyes sparkling against the blue glass as the ball twinkled and twirled. I let her admire its beauty, but when I put the car in gear, she gently put it back in the box. "We'll take good care of that, Brian, your own ornament for our tree. Right, we will be having Christmas in Linden Corners?"

Through the rearview mirror my eyes settled once again on the ornament. "Yes, Janey, and it will be a Christmas filled with fond memories for us both, and new traditions."

CHAPTER TWO

"Okay, Cyn, I'll see you in about an hour, thanks."

I set the phone back on the hook, glancing at the clock as I did so. It was two-thirty in the afternoon, Janey would be home from school within the hour, coinciding with when I had to leave to get the tavern set up for the night. This was the Thursday after Thanksgiving, usually not my night to work at George's, but the relief bartender I'd hired was running late and couldn't arrive until around six. So I'd asked my neighbor and friend Cynthia Knight if she wouldn't mind coming over to stay with Janey for a couple hours; she'd readily accepted. Cynthia had been Annie's best friend and could always be counted on in a pinch. I had been outside all morning, raking up the leaves that covered our land and, tired from the back-breaking work, I hopped into the shower, thinking how lucky I was to be surrounded by such caring people.

In fact, without Cynthia and her husband, Bradley, this new life of mine might never have been possible. Since the time of the terrible storm that had claimed our precious Annie, the Knights had been invaluable. Bradley, though a tax lawyer by trade, had helped take care of the legalities (along with an associate from his firm who handled complex family court issues) and a few weeks after Janey's eighth birthday, legal guardianship of her had been granted to me by the Columbia County Family Court down in Hudson. A short hearing, testimony from several of the residents of Linden Corners—Cynthia, Gerta, the gang at the Five O' Diner, even Father Burton over at St. Matthew's—had helped in my endeavor to keep Janey living at the farmhouse, inside the only home she'd ever known. Annie had also left instructions behind, proving to be the most powerful testimony in our petition. The courts couldn't ignore the overwhelming evidence set before them, that Janey Sullivan and Brian Duncan were the perfect match of child and guardian.

But the legal issue was only one matter, and a technical one, because the actual daily caring for Janey was even bigger, and it had been frightening and rewarding all at the same time. Since September, I had been trying to establish a set routine for Janey, knowing how important it was for me to be around as much as possible. I was awake each morning to get Janey ready for school, and on the weekends I was around all day, especially Sunday, which was the one day the tavern was closed, one of the many traditions I'd upheld after the death of its former owner, George Connors, Gerta's beloved husband. While I worked the late hours on Mondays and Fridays, Cynthia came over in the afternoons and stayed with Janey, and on Tuesdays and Saturdays, Gerta came over and did the same. Wednesday and Thursday was my time with Janey, days that I was always home, morning and night, believing an uninterrupted two-day stretch would give us some needed level of consistency. Today was the first day that our regular routine would be broken and I had to hope, as I toweled off in the upstairs bathroom after a refreshing shower, that Janey wouldn't object too much. She was usually good about change, usually so adaptable.

At three-fifteen I stepped off the porch, the cool afternoon air invigorating as I walked to the edge of the long driveway, where I saw that the school bus was just coming to a stop in front of the mailbox. Janey hopped off, as did her friend, Ashley, a fellow classmate from across Linden Corners. I suddenly remembered that Janey had asked if her friend could visit today.

I waved to the bus driver, and she waved back before driving to her next stop.

"Hi Brian," Janey said.

"Hi. Hello, Ashley."

"Hi, Mr. Duncan," she replied, her brown pig-tails bobbing from the mischievous bounce in her step.

"So, what are you girls planning to do today?"

"It's a secret," Janey said.

"Yeah, secret."

"Oh, so no boys allowed, huh?"

"Definitely not," Ashley commented, looking to Janey for confirmation. She nodded.

"Good, then you won't mind if Cynthia comes over for a couple hours? Mark's going to be late getting to the tavern so I need to get it set up."

Janey shrugged. "Oh, okay," she said, then scrunched up her face. Which meant she had a question to ask.

"What is it, Janey?"

"Can I show your pretty name ornament to Ashley? I was telling her about it and, how I wished that I..." She didn't finish her statement. "Can I?"

I said okay, but reminded her...

"I know, be careful. I will, thanks. Bye."

And then she and her pig-tailed friend went dashing up the driveway, where on the front lawn they saw the giant piles of leaves I'd worked so hard to gather. The two of them leaped into one of them, spewing crisp yellow leaves all over the lawn. I informed them that when they were finished they could find the rakes in the barn and clean up. Ashley stuck her tongue out at me. Gee, sweet kid. I hoped not too bad an influence on Janey.

Cynthia Knight arrived a few minutes later, walking over the hill that separated her farm from the Sullivan farmhouse, bringing with her a fresh bag of apples. As the local purveyor of quality fruits and vegetables, Cynthia managed a little stand on the outskirts of town, while her husband, Bradley, worked as a lawyer up in Albany; the two of them were an attractive and all too nice couple in their early thirties. I couldn't imagine my life without either of them.

"Thanks, Cyn, I owe you one."

"No debts here, remember?"

"Sure," I said. "If I'm going to be later than seven, I'll call."

As I hopped into my car, I yelled over to Janey, asked her over.

"What's up?" she asked.

"Did you just say 'What's up'?"

"Ashley says it all the time," she informed me.

"Well, how about next time you try, 'yes, what is it?'" Annie had been a stickler for Janey speaking proper English, full sentences accompanied by polite demeanor, and usually that's just what you got. I was trying to keep alive the same rules. "So, you okay with this? With me going to the tavern? This is usually our time."

"It's okay, Brian, you have your life, too," she said, then without knowing if she was dismissed, she bounded off to the backyard, Ashley chasing after her but unable to catch up. It was amazing how fast Janey ran, the distance between us so far, so fast, maybe more than I realized.

Since returning from my parents', I had begun to notice a slight change in Janey's behavior. Nothing drastic, just little actions or phrases that if you wanted to scrutinize could account for a slight tremor in our delicate foundation. She starting to pick out her own clothes, she opting to fix her own breakfast in the morning, and today, her indifference to my breaking our well-established routine. Maybe it was just the excitement of having her friend over, but I was left with a feeling that Janey was somehow trying to assert her independence, as though my presence wasn't always needed. The idea that Janey would outgrow me, tire of me, those sorts of paranoid fantasies tended only to penetrate my thoughts in the late hours, and here they were, coming to me during the daylight hours. Fears no longer afraid of the power of the sun.

I headed to town, my stomach nervous and unsettled.

* * *

Linden Corners was a tiny village located in Columbia County, New York, a hop and a skip from the mighty Hudson River, and boasted a population of just over seven hundred close-knit people. Route 23 was the main road that cut through the downtown section of the village, where small shops and even smaller restaurants lined each side of the street, those and a small park that was rimmed by trees, a white-trimmed gazebo in the center of its green lawn. Down the road was St. Matthew's Church, a cemetery adjacent to it; up one of the side roads was the Methodist Church and in nearby towns Hillside and Craryville were other places of worship, along with even better services, fancier dining establishments and several antique stores that catered to the renowned tourist trade. In Linden Corners, we liked to think of ourselves as self-sufficient, able to meet everyone's needs, from Marla and Darla's Trading Post and Groceries, to Chuck Ackroyd's hardware emporium and Martha Martinson's Five O'clock Diner; and of course, across from Ackroyd's, the formerly named Connors' Corner, now rechristened as George's Tavern. It was George's I was most familiar with. The tavern was on the main floor and on the upper floor, an apartment where I lived when I'd first come to town.

With Thanksgiving having slipped by, the calendar had just turned to December. So many of the townsfolk had begun to decorate their buildings with colorful lights and adorn their windows with Christmas pictures and banners, lighting up the village for the holiday season that would soon be thrust upon us. As evening began to descend over the sky, I was reminded that I needed to do something festive with the tavern, I couldn't be outdone by the others business owners, not with this being my first year here. Approaching the building, I made a mental note to ask Gerta where George might have kept any decorations he'd used. And then I pulled into the parking lot adjacent to the tavern, getting out and waving across the street to Martha Martinson, the stout, fiftysomething proprietor of the Five O. She was up on a ladder hanging her own string of lights.

"Better hurry with that," I said, "it's getting darker earlier."

"Just looking at that lonely bar of yours, that'll darken anything," Martha said, her good nature in tact, her humor typically off-kilter.

The Five O'—officially Martha's Five O'clock Diner, because those were its peak feeding times, a.m. and p.m.—was the first place I'd ever stopped at in Linden Corners—the windmill notwithstanding—and both Martha and a waitress named Sara had welcomed me with unaccustomed friendliness; they had ended up changing my life. Because my lunch-time visit became an overnight stay and then I stayed another night, and soon after found myself gainfully employed, and all of it I took to be evidence that I was meant to be drawn in by the power of this unique village, by its residents and by the windmill that seemed to speak to them, inspire them. It had done so with me, still did.

Martha was right, the bar did look abandoned, and so I hurried up the steps, unlocked the door and immediately flicked on the overhead lights, yellow beams illuminating the large room. I turned on the jukebox—Guster's "Keep it Together"—and in short order I had transformed the quiet bar into a welcoming beacon off the highway. Mark had left the place in good shape from the night before, but still I went through my routine, cleaning the tables and wiping down the chairs and the long oak bar, too, polishing the brass with a sense of pride that I'd learned first-hand from George. I checked the taps to make sure they were working, beer being the bread and butter of my business. Everything was in working order, I was ready for my first customers.

The sun went down early this December day, and by four-thirty dusk had settled over Linden Corners, headlights flashing by as the early-rising residents returned to their homes for the night. Fortunately, a few of them stopped off for a drink, and by five o'clock seven of the bar stools were taken and beers were laid out in front of them, a couple of the guys already asking for refills after their hard day's work. A young couple had arrived as well, opting to take a table, and when I served them their drinks I set a bowl of pretzels in front of them.

So all was under control, giving me a chance to relax behind the great oak bar, to immerse myself in this still-new world of mine. Janey's comment about my having my own life popped into my mind and I wondered if there was any truth to that. Since September I had felt that my life—my goals and my ambitions—was on hold as I focused all my concentration on Janey. She needed it and I wanted to. After nearly three months I had no doubts that I was doing the right thing, I had made a promise to Annie and one to Janey, too, and given the circumstances I was happy to fulfill them, wishing still and always that the circumstances weren't what they were. Annie should be with us both—today, yesterday, tomorrow, sharing the joy we tried to find in each little moment of every day. Instead, Janey and I survived together, my routine dictated by hers, certainly a big change from where I'd been even a year ago. Living in New York, obsessed with its frenetic pace, its lures to the good life, its easy seductions.

My reverie was interrupted by the arrival of another customer; she was the waitress from the Five-O and not one of my regulars. I said hello, asked her what brought her here.

"Hi, Bri. Looking for Mark," she said, sidling up the bar.

"He's running late," I said, curiously suspicious why she was asking after Mark Ravens. "So you're stuck with me, that okay?"

She shrugged. "Guess I'll have to live with it."

Sara, a pretty blonde, was twenty-two, had grown up in Linden Corners and unlike many of her classmates, she didn't seem eager to leave town. She liked her job, liked her friends, and from what I gathered from her expression now, she liked my relief bartender.

"He should be here soon, why not have a seat."

"Thanks. Gimme a Coors Light."

"Watching your girlish figure?" I asked.

"No one else is," she replied, chuckling as she did. "Martha would have liked that one."

Martha and Sara, in addition to serving some of the best food in the area, both liked to joke around at the customer's expense. Sara's humor was improving, since when I first met her the conversation had been laced with roadkill remarks, not exactly what you wanted to hear from a diner waitress.

"The Five-O looks good," I said, pointing out the window. Martha had finished putting up the lights and the perimeter of the diner was glowing with holiday lights, reds and greens and blues enlivening the bustling activity at the diner. It was, after all, just past five in the afternoon, the dinner rush.

As Sara sipped at her beer, I asked why she wasn't working, and she explained that Thursday was her day off, "which stinks, really, since it's one of Mark's busy days."

I nodded. "Didn't know you and Mark were so, uh, tight."

She easily grinned, and I needed no further indication she was smitten with him. "Yeah, well, I'd seen him around town, in school, even though he was a couple years ahead of me. He never gave me the time of day, not until I brought him over a dinner plate a few weeks ago. It was a slow night both here and at the diner. He invited me over for a drink after work, and I did and well, we've gone out a couple times."

"Good for you."

"You know it," she said with confidence.

As I went to serve another customer, I laughed.

Mark Ravens was a local kid who worked during the day down in Hudson, waiting tables himself for one of the finer resort hotels, but he'd been looking for some extra cash and I'd been looking for a relief bartender, and his uncle, Richie, who ran the only motel in Linden Corners, the Solemn Nights, had recommended him. One meeting was all it had taken, we shook hands, agreed on the hours and wage and ever since then bar receipts were great on the nights he worked; point of fact, he brought in the ladies, evidenced by Sara's presence here tonight. Why not, he was younger, and in some patrons' words, "hotter." Those customer tended not to get a buy back from me.

I refilled a couple more glasses and then, encouraged by the decorations up at the Five-O, I phoned Gerta Connors to ask after Christmas decorations for the tavern and learned that George did have some, he kept them in the attic of their home, did I want to come over some night soon and look for them. We agreed on Sunday.

"Perfect, thanks."

"Come for dinner, bring Janey," Gerta insisted.

At five minutes after six the door opened and with a blast of wind in walked my relief bartender. Mark Ravens was just below my height, five ten and at twenty-four, he grew his wavy dark hair long and today he was sporting an unshaven look. He smiled at the sight of Sara, then apologized for being late.

"One of the evening waiters didn't show up, they needed me to stay and at least set-up for the dinner crowd."

"No problem, Cynthia's with Janey. Speaking of, now that you're here I'll hand over the reigns to you and head on back to the farmhouse."

"Okay, later Windmill Man," Mark said, tying an apron around his waist while he leaned in for a kiss from Sara. "Hey, babe."

A few other cars had turned into the parking lot and more ladies joined the action that was becoming a town attraction, George's Tavern on a Thursday night. This bar, it just might make some money and I wouldn't need that check from my father, the check that I'd stashed—uncashed—in a desk drawer. Then I left my business in good hands, a smile on my face. I was glad to know that Mark and Sara had found each other, that happiness was spreading in the village of Linden Corners. That even as winter descended upon us, there was still the chance for love to bloom.

* * *

When I got home, Ashley had already gone home to her parents and Janey was up in her room doing her homework, giving me and Cynthia a moment to talk.

"How was she tonight?"

"Fine, as always," Cynthia said, "You know I would have called if there had been anything wrong."

"Her mood? Attitude, no problems?"

"None. Brian, what's going on?"

Maybe nothing, I thought, dismissing my concerns as pure paranoia. "Forget it," I said.

Cynthia was unconvinced but let it pass, knowing that I'd open up if there was truly something seriously amiss. She gave me a quick hug, and then said she'd better get back on home, "Bradley was working late but he's probably home; I hope he started dinner. Gotta love the modern man. See you."

"Thanks, Cyn."

I went upstairs and said hi to Janey, who waved at me, her face buried in her math textbook. When I asked if she needed help, she just waved me away without even bothering to look up. Feeling dejected, I went back downstairs and tooled around for another hour, until bedtime arrived. When I returned to her room, she was already in her pajamas, under the covers and reading a book, her stuffed purple frog on one side, a new plush puppy on the other; she was reading aloud to them both.

"Did you brush your teeth?"

"Of course, Brian. I know how to get myself ready for bed."

"I know. I just like to check anyway, okay?"

I sat down on the edge of her bed, feeling like a stranger all of sudden. Janey, who had been looking and acting so grown up lately, now in her pink pajamas she appeared to be that sweet little girl I'd met at the base of the windmill, the one who'd been afraid of nothing. I wondered if something was frightening her, and I asked her if everything was okay.

"Yes."

"You'd tell me otherwise?"

"Yes, Brian," she said, her usual exasperation missing; tonight there was a distance to her voice.

"I love you tons, Janey Sullivan," I said, my voice suddenly failing me. I waited a moment at the door, then said, "Good-night. Don't forget to turn out the light when you've finished reading to your animals."

As I readied to leave the room, she called out to me, causing me to turn quickly, hoping that whatever was bothering her was about to be revealed.

"Who was Lucy?"

"Lucy?"

"Yeah, that woman you almost married, the one your sister talked about at Thanksgiving. Did you love her?"

This wasn't something to be dealt with in the doorway. I returned to her side, sitting on the edge of the bed but not getting too close. "Her name is Lucy Watkins. What she and I had, well, that was a long time ago, when I was just a college kid and so was she and we didn't know any better. I didn't know what true love really was."

"Do you know now?"

I smiled at her when I said, "You bet I do."

"Brian?"

"Yeah, sweetie?"

"Why did you come to Linden Corners?"

Why. That was a good question, one I hadn't been even been able to answer when Annie had asked me that very same thing. Did I even know how to answer it myself? Sometimes you don't know why you do things, you just follow your instinct, follow the past that destiny has laid out for you. But neither of these arbitrary answers would suit the very grounded Janey Sullivan, and so I said to her, "You want to know the God's-honest truth, Janey? I really don't know why I came to Linden Corners, I had never even heard of it until, well, until I practically drove right through it. You want to know another truth?"

She nodded.

"I do know why I stayed."

This time she smiled. "Ashley really liked your ornament, Brian."

"I'm glad," I said. "You put it back in the attic?"

She didn't look at me, instead focused her attention on the purple frog. "See what I have to put up with?" she told him.

I laughed, then gave Janey a kiss on the forehead. On my way out I turned off the light. No more books, I said, time for sleep, and she accepted my decision easily, sliding beneath the covers and closing her eyes. Me, I retreated back to the living room more confused than ever. For so many weeks, bedtime had gone smoothly, she and I talking any problems out with ease, with little riddle to our conversations. Tonight, though, Janey had knocked me over with her questions about Lucy, a girl I'd not given much thought to in many years. I supposed it wasn't Lucy she was actually curious about, maybe it was the discovery that there had been someone in my life before her mother, instilling in her the notion that before coming to Linden Corners, I had had my own life. A different life. And one that hadn't included her.

CHAPTER THREE

Saturday night I kept the tavern open longer than usual, until two a.m., and there was a good reason for it—there was nothing waiting for me back at the farmhouse. Janey had asked to have a sleepover at Ashley's and I saw no reason why not, so off she went with her overnight bag and off I went with a full night of work ahead at George's. It was a busy night, with my regulars outnumbered by a group of out of towners who were attending an antiques show. Regardless of who was from where, they were all looking for something to occupy their time for a few hours, a place where they could leave their troubles behind. Apparently they had either lots of time to kill or lots of problems to forget, because as midnight came and went, they all stayed, and the taps kept up with them, until one forty-five when I announced last call. The last straggler finished his beer at two-fifteen and as he ventured out into the cold early morning air, I locked the door behind him and set about cleaning up the messy bar. A half-hour later I turned off the lights and left, George's Tavern closed until Monday at four p.m.

Linden Corners was quiet as I drove along the empty roads, my headlights guiding me in the darkness. There was a noticeable chill in the air, snow was in the forecast, as it had been for most of the last couple of weeks. Aside from some harmless flurries, nothing much had accumulated. The weatherman continued to spout those same predictions each night, I guess figuring he'd be right eventually. I was about to make the turn off onto Crestview Road and head home, but instead continued straight on Route 23 until I saw the windmill. My headlights caught sight of the sails of the windmill, which were anything but dormant in these early hours of the new day, the wind having picked up the past couple of hours. Like I had done so often during my first few weeks in Linden Corners, I pulled to the side of the road, keeping the beams of light focused on the windmill. Sitting atop the roof of my car—in a case of turnabout is fair play, Annie had called it Brian's Bluff—I gazed forward, wrapping my arms around myself for warmth.

And I thought.

I thought about holidays and I thought about traditions and I thought about Janey and what was best for her. I thought about tomorrow, which was already today by the turn of the clock, knowing Janey and I would be spending the entire day together, a typical Sunday for us. But thinking, too, would it really be so typical, because our time together of late had been anything but. I thought about what we might do, what I might say, to somehow bring us back to the even footing that had been the foundation of our relationship. Then, as the chill began to seep beneath my clothes and prickle at my skin, I thought maybe I was thinking too much.

Silently, I said goodnight to Annie, watching as the snow flakes began to fall right then and there, caught in the glow of the headlights, the early strokes of a winter portrait.

When I returned to the farmhouse, I didn't turn on any lamps as I made my way through each room with easy familiarity, a sign that I'd become comfortable within these once-foreign walls. I changed into sweats and left my bedroom, taking a moment to look in Janey's empty room, her purple frog alone on the freshly-made bed. I retreated then to the warmth of the living room. No television, no music, no noise, just the quiet sounds of late night. I found myself staring out the window; it was snowing heavily now and if this continued there was a good chance of waking to a blanket of snow covering the land.

I tossed a blanket over myself and again my mind toyed with my emotions. In the wake of Annie being gone, visiting with her spirit at the base of the windmill generally brought me calm. Tonight it had brought about the reverse, Janey's momma had evaded me, almost as though she was siding these days with her fickle-minded daughter. An image of Annie's late husband, Dan Sullivan, popped into my head and I wondered whether his spirit moved across the land, too, did he ever visit the place he'd called home. No matter what else happened between me and Janey, good and bad, there was no denying the truth. I was an impostor, a substitute for the people who had given her life. Who had, in a moment of consuming love, made her the magical girl she was. At Thanksgiving Katrina Henderson had made a misjudgment by referring to me as Janey's Dad. Maybe I had made the bigger mistake, thinking I could possibly fulfill that duty, if not in name than in spirit.

At last, I closed my eyes, and drifted off to sleep, the first time I'd ever slept alone in the Sullivan farmhouse. No Sullivans in sight.

* * *

We had eight inches of fresh white snow by morning,

and thanks to a wave of cold air that continued to flow through the countryside, none of the snow threatened to melt anytime soon. In fact, the top layer was crunchy as our boots stomped over it. It was the first measurable snow of the season, so Janey and I had decided to take full advantage of winter's arrival, dragging the sled out of the barn—dusting it off first—and then making good use of the hill in the our expansive backyard. Janey's face lit up from the fun she was having, the sled cutting through the wind as it raced downward. My job was simple: walk the sled back up the hill so she could go again. After about ten trips, I said, "Hey, when is it my turn?"

"What do you mean?" she asked, her face masked by a hat and scarf.

"Come on, give me the sled."

"Silly, Brian. Grown-ups don't go sledding."

"Shows what you know," I said, taking hold of the reigns of the sled. I climbed aboard it, trying to fit my six foot frame on the red toboggan that wasn't made for me—for "grown ups." Sitting upright first, my feet stretched far over the front; that didn't work. Then I tried to sit cross-legged, but my knees were like wings on an airplane, but unable to take flight. Finally, I laid down on my stomach, my legs dangling over the back of the sled.

Janey found much to be amused about. "Brian, you won't get very far."

"Oh yeah?" I said, teasingly.

"Yeah."

"Watch this," was my final comment, and that's when I gave myself a good, hearty push. Suddenly, I was hurtling down the hill on a direct course with the windmill, Janey taking up the chase behind me, her happy screams somehow fueling the sled to more power. But then I decided the ride had gone on long enough and I turned the sled over and allowed myself to crash into the snow. As I rolled to a stop and feigned unconsciousness, Janey came over to check on me. That's when I grabbed her ankles and pulled her down. She let out a quick yelp as I did so.

"Brian, stop, Brian, come on...that tickles…" she stated in mock protest. As we wrestled, she grabbed a handful of snow and rolled it into a hard-packed ball. As I tried to escape its wrath, she threw the snowball. It landed square on my chest, and, keeping the game alive, I fell to the ground like a soldier in battle. But this didn't stop the assault, as she continued to pound me with snowballs. I buried my head with my arms, waiting for just the right moment to spring my surprise on her. Quickly, I grabbed some snow and stood up, hurling it at her. She let out another peel of laughter while she retreated up the hill. I started after her.

"No, you have to bring the sled back up," she said as I closed in on her. "No fair, you're too big, you'll catch me easily."

So I went back for the sled, and while I did she reached the top of the hill. When I returned, she planted another snowball on me, grabbing the sled as I ducked. In seconds she had leaped onto the sled and was making her escape down the hill, laughing as the distance between us grew. "Ha, ha, Brian, I won, I won."

So I let her win, because it had been days since I'd seen her this happy, since she and I had had such a good time. And even though I was chilled to the bone, I wanted nothing more than for this sweet moment to last forever. I settled for another hour, and then we went back inside the farmhouse to warm up. Her cheeks and the tip of her nose were a rosy red.

"Hey, Rudolph," I said, "how about some hot chocolate."

"Yeah, yeah, with marshmallows."

"I'll see if we've got any."

"We always have them. Momma never lets us run out..."

In a flash, Janey had quieted down and run from the kitchen. I wanted to go after her, but decided not to press the issue, not now, not after we'd had such a joyous time. Instead, I made the hot chocolate, adding some Hershey's chocolate syrup to make it extra flavorful. As it cooled, I looked inside the cabinets and pulled out a half-empty bag of mini-marshmallows, probably left over from some summer picnic. I tossed a bunch of them in each mug, and then brought them both up to her room, resting on a tray that also had some lemon cookies for dunking. Janey was sitting on the floor and I joined her, leaning against the bed.

"I'm sorry, Brian."

"You have nothing to apologize for. Janey, there's going to be a lot of moments like that, things that will remind you of your mother. I want you to remember them and most importantly, I want you to talk about them. I want to hear about every single one of them. You'll feel sad, that's natural, but if you think about how much your mother enjoyed them, especially when you shared in her enjoyment, well, you'll start to remember all the wonderful times you had with her."

She sniffled, and I reached for one of the napkins on the tray. She wiped her dripping nose, then took hold of the mug. She took a sip, then smiled.

"Extra-chocolatey."

"You told me that's the way you liked it."

"Actually, that wasn't me," she said. "It was Momma who liked it with the chocolate sauce. And it's real yummy, thanks, Brian. It's my favorite way now."

We sat in companionable silence as we sipped at our hot chocolate and emptied the tray of cookies, both of us even picking up the crumbs with the tips of our fingers. I showed her how to get the maximum amount of crumbs by dampening the fingertips. Janey again informed me I was silly, but that only made this day even more special, knowing she and I had recaptured the magic that had defined our relationship.

As she set down her mug, she wiped away a chocolate mustache. "Hey, Brian, can I ask you a question?"

"Anything, you know that."

"Are we going to get a tree?"

"A tree? You mean a Christmas tree? Of course."

"When?"

"When would like to get it?"

"What day is it?"

"It's Sunday."

"No, the date."

"Oh, it's December fourth, a Sunday."

"In two weeks, I think. Momma and I, we would always go and cut down a tree in the middle of December, so we could have the tree decorated for a while. You remember I told you that at Thanksgiving? I like to see it all lit up, with that shiny stuff."

"Tinsel?"

"That's it. So, can we? You know, get the tree?"

"Consider it done," I told her.

"Why should we pretend it's done? What's the fun in that? Chopping the tree down is almost the best part."

I smiled. "You know, it's going to take me a little while to get used to all your traditions, Janey."

"I can help."

"How?"

"Follow me."

She left her room and went down to the end of the hall, where she opened the door that led to the musty attic. Trailing behind her, I flicked on the attic light to guide our way up. It was cold up here, but Janey seemed impervious to it, determined now in her mission that nothing could stop her. Amidst the sea of boxes that contained the Sullivan family history—and before them, the history of the Van Diver family, who had built the farmhouse and the windmill—were several boxes marked "X-mas" in hand-writing I recognized as Annie's. Even deep in the attic, where the past came alive, we felt her presence.

As I pulled the boxes aside, Janey tore off the tops, revealing a burst of decorations, lights and balls and other trinkets that would be set on, if not the tree itself, then the fireplace mantel or on the walls or upon the doors. There was also an envelope marked "pictures," and when I opened it, I discovered they were of a Christmas past. Annie in her bathrobe, Janey is hers, the two of them surrounded by gifts and discarded wrapping paper. Janey squealed in delight, telling me these were from last year, she knew, because that's when she had gotten the sled, the one we had been using today.

"I remember, because last Christmas there was no snow and so I couldn't use it," she said. "I guess Momma never had time to put these in a photo album. Look, there's one of Cynthia and Bradley, they came over last year, I remember that, too. See, Bradley took that picture of Momma and Cynthia. And that's me...."

Janey and I sat there for a good long time, poring over each photograph, me listening to the story that accompanied each one, making mental notes to myself about things to incorporate into our upcoming celebration. Then, as she put the photos back, Janey suddenly grew excited again as she began pulling off the top of another box. She clapped wildly when she made her discovery.

"Brian, you'll love this, I know you will," she said.

She had pulled out what must have been Annie's most favorite Christmas decoration, a ceramic, snow-covered windmill, complete with sails that actually spun. Carefully, Janey handed it to me and I gazed lovingly on it, mesmerized by its simple beauty. I asked Janey if we could bring this one downstairs now and she clapped at the suggestion.

"It's never too early for Christmas," she said.

"No, not in the land of the windmill it's not."

Just then the telephone rang, and Janey went racing to answer it, leaving me in the attic alone. I started to get up, then changed my mind. I knew in one of these nearby boxes were photo albums from years ago, and when I found them—four of them—I started to look through them, hunting for other clues to Christmas traditions of the past. And I stumbled upon an album that turned out to contain memories of Janey's first Christmas, she just eleven weeks old, Annie holding her as she sat in front of the Christmas tree. No doubt her husband, Dan, had taken the photo. As an answer to my question, the next photo was of Dan, now holding Janey as a smile lit his handsome face. Emotion swelled within me, blocked in my throat. My God, what forces of nature had brought this precious little girl to this moment, only eight and planning her future holidays without either of these needed people in her life. How fortunate I was to be caring for her, but how daunting a task it was too. Suddenly feeling like I was intruding on a history I had no business knowing, I put the photo albums back. But in that cold musty attic that day, I made a vow—to Annie? To Dan Sullivan, too?—that I would do all I could to make this holiday perfect for Janey. But how? I knew she would need the most special gift possible.

When Janey returned to the attic, she scrunched her nose at me. "Hey, come on, that was Gerta, we're having dinner with her, remember?"

I had remembered, but I hadn't realized how much time had gotten away from us. It was closing in on five in the afternoon. I asked Janey to give me a couple more minutes, as I realized something was wrong, or more accurately, something was missing. I had placed the box which contained my family ornament in the near corner, by the staircase. Today, though, it wasn't there.

"Janey, did you show Ashley my ornament?"

"Yes, oh, Brian, her eyes just lit up with jealousy, remember I told you. You're very forgetful lately. I could see the blue glass in her eyes, that's how pretty it is."

"Where did you find it?"

She turned and pointed to the exact location I had placed it. "Hey, where's the box?"

"That's a good question," I said. "Are you sure you didn't leave it in your room?"

Janey nodded, her lips starting to quiver. "Uh-huh. I put it right back there."

She was getting upset and after the great day we'd had I didn't want to jeopardize her mood. And so I said let's forget about it, it must be somewhere among the other boxes.

"I'll find it later, Janey," I said. "No big deal."

* * *

Gerta Connors lived on the other side of the village of Linden Corners, in a house she had shared with her husband, George, for nearly fifty years, a home that had seen four girls grow from infants to adults while surrounded by lots of love and some of the best cooking I'd ever tasted. Tonight was no exception, as Gerta prided herself on her home-cooked meals, and, as she explained, "I don't get much opportunity these days, so I welcome the chance." She had made a turkey breast and stuffing and vegetables, and said for dessert there was a strawberry pie, her specialty and one of my new favorite sweets; folks in Linden Corners, they knew their pies I had said on more than one occasion.

"It's like Thanksgiving all over again," Janey had said.

I think that had been deliberate on Gerta's part, the choice in meal. I had told her of the events of the Duncan family holiday, and I think she wanted to give Janey a chance to celebrate Thanksgiving in a place that was closer to her mother's heart. Well, I had told Gerta mostly what had happened, leaving out details such as the monetary gift from my father. Anyway, we feasted and then I helped clean up, while Janey went into the living room to watch television. That gave me and Gerta an opportunity to talk.

"How are you doing," I asked her, drying a pan.

"Oh, Brian, you know me. I get by."

"With a little help from your friends," I said, quoting the Beatles, realizing though how true that was for us all. "That's the good thing about Linden Corners, we help each other out. I don't know what I'd do without you all, you and Cynthia and Bradley. Heck, even Mark, having him take some of my hours at the tavern has made a huge difference. Janey and I, we need that time together."

"Well, of course you do," Gerta said. "Now, Brian, are you making enough money at the bar, you know, to be paying Mark? I know you're not paying him a lot and you rely on tips a lot, but you've got such responsibilities now. It's not just the amount of time you spend with Janey, but how you can provide for her."

"You sound like my father," I said, deciding it might be a good idea to share what he'd done for me. Get a second opinion on what I should do with it. "He gave me a check for twenty-five thousand dollars. At Thanksgiving, said it was his way of helping."

"Wow—that's very generous."

"But I don't want to accept it, Gerta. I realize what a help it would be, but..."

"You'll figure out what's right."

"Just not now," I said. "Once we get through the holidays, then I'll start to figure out the future. You know, New Year, new life. I've often thought that I need to find myself some other form of employment; more regular hours and better pay. The question is, what—and where. Don't get me wrong, Gerta, I love running the bar, the sense of freedom it gives me. But in reality, it's probably not the most suitable job to have given my current circumstances."

Gerta finished loading the dirty dishes into the dishwasher, then poured in some soap. "Has Janey said anything about it?"

"No. But I'm not sure she would. Janey's a wonder, some days I'm amazed at how composed she is, how resilient. But if something's bothering her, she's more apt to shut down. She reacts by not reacting. Last night, she had her first sleepover since...since Annie died, and all night long, both at the bar and when I returned home, I couldn't concentrate on anything, not the customers or on falling asleep. I think part of me was waiting for the phone to ring, and it would be Ashley's mother asking that I come and get Janey. But the call never came, and I can't figure out whether I was glad or sad."

"I think you didn't like rattling around that farmhouse all by yourself."

"I kept the bar open until two a.m, got home after three."

"Oh, Brian."

We had finished with the dishes and Janey was absorbed in the movie, so Gerta escorted me upstairs to the attic so I could find the decorations I had come for. My second attic visit, this one went quicker because I easily found the box marked "Corner X-mas" and there was no history lesson behind it. I carried the box downstairs and loaded it into my trunk, returning to the kitchen to find coffee and slices of strawberry pie set out on plates. Janey had hers already as the movie headed into its final half hour, and so I sat opposite Gerta at the kitchen table. I took a bite, the sweet berry flavor bursting inside my mouth, the luscious juice taking me back to the summer. To the Memorial Day picnic that had signaled a distinct, upward change in my relationship with Annie. Gerta saw the smile on my face and said, "You're welcome." I had a second slice.

"You know, Gerta, I could use some help at the tavern tomorrow during the day. Martha Martinson's been giving me such a hard time about the bar's lack of decorations, I've got to get them up as soon as possible. Maybe you can show me the way George used to hang the lights, decorate the outside."

"If you like," she said, surprisingly non-committal for her. When I called her on it, she confessed that too much of our lives were already mired in the past. "Decorate the bar the way you want, Brian, it's yours."

"No, Gerta," I said, shaking my head. "I'm merely the barkeep."

"You're not merely anything, Brian Duncan Just Passing Through."

I laughed at the mention of my old nickname. "Hey, that name's been retired."

"Nothing's ever retired, Brian," she said. "Things, they just lay dormant, waiting for the right time to come back. Like spring, it'll be back."

"After a long winter."

"Yup, Winter's Just Passing Through."

"Like traditions," I said, my mind suddenly thinking about my own family. About my parents and their desire to not spend Christmas alone in their new home. Of my sister, Rebecca, who seemed equally adrift during the holidays, running from relationship to relationship. And what of myself, was I ready to leave behind the traditions I had known? I thought of the ornament that was mysteriously missing, and that unlocked in my memory banks pictures of my brother, Philip. He'd been the oldest of the three of us, twelve years senior to me. A championship athlete, he had had the world at his feet.

Gerta was right, nothing goes away forever. Not things we think we lost, that we forgot. Certainly not memories, they rise back to the surface when you least expect them.

"You still with us, Brian?"

I looked up and found a curious Gerta staring at me. "Oh, sorry, I was...daydreaming."

Janey had just entered the kitchen with her dirty plate. "It's nighttime, Brian, you can't daydream at night."

We did the last of the dishes and thanked Gerta for her hospitality and wonderful food, and then bade her good-night.

Janey and I returned home shortly after nine o'clock and she fell fast asleep, exhausted from our very full day. I retired to the living room, where my eyes feasted upon the ceramic windmill I'd taken down from the attic. Again, my mind whirled with thoughts, about Janey, about the wonderful day that had just passed, about the two of us seemingly over the hump that had impeded us this week. And I thought about Annie, too, feeling her spirit by the mere presence of the windmill ornament. That night, I slept better, feeling as though there were two Sullivans at my side.

But, alas, no Duncans.

CHAPTER FOUR

Even though I had been living at the farmhouse since September my New York friend John Oliver chose never to call me there, opting to phone me only at George's Tavern. And his calls usually came during the day, which meant the company he theoretically worked for was paying for the call, not him; and he could seemingly talk for as long as he wanted. Ten o'clock that next morning, it appeared John had all the time in the world to spare.

"They expect me to wake up after a whole weekend of playing and just start working right away?" John was saying, and when I had no response for him, he asked, rhetorically, "I mean, whatever happened to easing you way into your work week?"

I answered anyway. "Maybe you can ask them if you can have Mondays off."

"Nah, that would only mean I'd have to go through the same ordeal each Tuesday," he said. "Man, it's just mornings, they're killers. I can't imagine what it's like to get up and have to milk cows before the sun comes up. How do you do it, farmer-boy?"

John truly believed I was a farmer. It was nice to know he hadn't changed one bit since I'd left the city.

We chatted back and forth for a good twenty minutes and when the topic switched over to the weather, I informed John that I had work to do, and, well, whether "there's a point to this phone call?"

"Yeah, I was wondering, am I going to see you this month? You know, are you coming down to the city anytime soon? I mean, it's been too long."

Frankly, I hadn't given it any thought. I had closed the chapter of my life that was New York City months ago, and aside from occasional thoughts of its steel canyons and its crazy pace and its memories both good and bad, the city that once kept my pulse racing had faded once put on life support; like another life, lived a lifetime ago. Still, I had to wonder why John was asking, and so taking the direct approach—which was always best when dealing with him—I was surprised nonetheless by his answer.

"I'm in love."

Good thing I wasn't cleaning a glass when he made that pronouncement. I might be picking up shards from the floor. "Uh, you want to repeat that? I think we've got a bad connection."

"Hey, it happens to you all the time, Bri, why not me?"

"Because you're the kind of guy who thinks love is a four-letter word."

"It is," he replied.

"That's not exactly what I meant."

"Brian, she's amazing. Come on, man, drop on down for a weekend, we'll revisit all the old haunts, maybe even find you a nice girl..."

"You're forgetting one thing."

"What's that?"

"A certain eight year old girl named Janey," I said. "John, I can't just go running off to New York on a whim. I have responsibilities, people who count on me, and I'm not just talking about Janey. As it is, she and I only get one day a week to ourselves and that's precious time..." Suddenly a random thought popped into my mind, cutting off my own speech. I considered it quickly as silence ate up the phone line. Then I said, "What are you doing next Sunday?"

"This coming Sunday? I don't know, it's only Monday."

"Keep it free."

"We going bar-hopping?"

"No. You say you're in love, well, I want to meet the woman in your life. And John, I want you to meet the one in mine. Though mine is an eight-year-old girl who will charm your socks off."

"Mine charms off more than that," he said.

"Ew," I said.

Still, I laughed at John's juvenile joke, reassured that his proclamation of love hadn't affected his sense of humor. We talked a few more minutes about possible scenarios for the coming weekend's visit and then we signed off with a laugh, John getting in one last dig about the farmer lifestyle he thought I'd adapted to.

"You got to visit the henhouse now?" he asked.

"You're the one with a woman in his life," I retorted.

"Nice, farmer boy."

"I am not a farmer," I exclaimed into the phone. It was no use, he'd hung up already, no doubt dialing another long-distance call. Heck, it wasn't yet noon, how could he be expected to be working?

As for me, there was a lot of work ahead of me, notably the Christmas decorations to be put around the outside of the tavern. This morning I had loaded the box I'd taken from Gerta's attic into Annie's old truck, and placed alongside it a ladder and a staple gun I'd found among the tools in the barn. I headed out to the porch, buttoning up against the cold air, and began the task at hand. The string of lights was plenty and after an hour's work I had barely made a dent. A co-worker would been helpful, but Mark was at his other job today. I would have taken anyone at this point. At one point I found myself tangled in a mess of wires and when I tried to clear myself, I only made more of a mess of the situation. In other words, I lost my footing on the ladder and fell to the snow-covered ground. Quickly I brushed myself off and resumed my work, glad no one had seen what transpired. A few minutes later cars started to stop by the Five-O across the street, and I realized lunchtime was fast-approaching. I put down the staple gun, locked up the tavern and walked over to the diner, where I took a stool at the front counter.

"Hey, Brian, real sorry you stopped putting up those lights," Martha said, "though, we did have to get back to work. You put on a good show—lots of comedy. That plotz in the snow, loved it."

So much for no one witnessing my tumble from the ladder.

"Gee, didn't know you were that bored, Martha."

"Oh, anything for a laugh," she said.

"I know what you mean, I certainly don't come here for the cooking."

I heard a series of chuckles from the other customers, from Sara too, who was pouring me a cup of coffee.

"Good one, Bri," she said.

Martha, feigning injury to her pride, turned away from me. It wasn't often someone got the best of her and as good-natured as she was, she still wouldn't admit I'd gotten one over on her. She returned to the kitchen and Sara put in my order for a cheese and mushroom omelet. Ten minutes later Martha emerged from the kitchen with a steaming plate of food and set it before me, grinning as she did so.

"Come on, Windmill Man, take a bite."

"I don't trust you," I said, kiddingly. But I began to eat the hot food anyway while Martha stood over and watched.

After I'd taken a few safe bites, she leaned in and said, "So, Brian, you're setting up the Christmas lights just like George did, does this mean you'll be hosting the annual party too?"

"What party?"

"Week before Christmas, George Connors opened up the Corner for any and all, played Santa to us needy—and thirsty—children. Gerta gets busy too, sets out a nice buffet, something I always appreciated since it gave me a day off; a night, too. Can't tell you how many First Friday celebrations I was serving up meals at two in the morning after the close of his party. You drink a few, you get hungry. But the Christmas Party at the Corner, why that's a Connors tradition."

"No, I know nothing of it. Gerta's never said a word, not even when I was over there last night picking up the lights."

Martha shrugged. "Maybe it's not meant to be? It's a new year coming to Linden Corners and, well, we've seen a few too many changes come this past one, not many of which we're happy about."

I nodded, knowing exactly what she meant. We'd all lost people we'd loved, their deaths tragic, sorrowful, remorseful. And as difficult as loss was, at this time of year you couldn't help but recall them with a greater intensity. I was an expert at such feelings, it was a Duncan family trait. I would have expected Gerta to feel the same and that she would have mentioned the Christmas party to me. Could have been her way of remembering George by resurrecting one of his time-honored ways.

"Maybe a party is just what we all need," I said to Martha, who nodded in agreement.

"'Tis the season," Sara said, refilling my coffee cup.

"Just don't say anything, not just yet," I asked them both.

"Not a word," Martha agreed.

"But if we don't tell anyone, how will anyone know to come?" Sara asked.

"I mean let me do the telling," I said, wanting to run the idea first past Gerta anyway. She may have had her own reasons for saying nothing of George's traditions and if she wished to skip the party this year, I would respect her wishes.

I polished off my meal, leaving nary a crumb—"nothing for the mice" Martha liked to joke—and returned to the tavern, where, inspired by the spreading of holiday cheer, I attacked those darn lights with a vengeance, and before long they were all up, lining the porch and the outer trim of the house. It had been a major project, and thankfully I had it done before the sun had gone down. I had an hour to wait, actually, before true darkness fell and I did so with great impatience, ready to see my handiwork on display. At four-thirty, the colorful lights went on across at the Five-O, at the bank and down by Marla and Darla's twin stores. Linden Corners was suddenly a burst of reds and greens and oranges and blues, a holiday rainbow. I was ready to contribute to the village glow when a car pulled into the parking lot. It was Gerta.

"Oh good, I'm not too late."

"I was just about to turn them on," I told her. "Unless you'd like to do the honors."

"It's your bar," she said.

"So all decisions are mine?"

"Certainly, Brian."

I ran inside and flicked the switch and heard Gerta's gleeful exclamation. I dashed out, backing up to the sidewalk where Gerta stood. And there she and I admired the explosion of color that encircled George's Tavern, itself alive with the glow of a new life, new light.

"It's beautiful, Brian, like always. And just as we discussed last night, traditions can't be denied; they take on a power all their own. You've brought back George's redoubtable spirit, and I appreciate it so much. In fact, there's this other tradition George had..."

"And I hope you'll be able to make it," I said.

Gerta leaned into me and I hugged her. I sent a silent thank you Martha's way for the heads-up about the annual party; everyone in Linden Corners seemed to look out for one another. As the Christmas lights shed colorful shadows upon the snow, a tear trickled down Gerta's cheek.

"Oh my, I guess I have some cooking to do," she said, anticipation energizing her smile.

* * *

Cynthia and Bradley Knight lived half a mile away from the Sullivan farmhouse, just up Crestview Road on a farm of their own, where they grew an assortment of fruits and vegetables and sold them (in season) at their stand located just on the outskirts of Linden Corners. It was

Wednesday, just two days after I'd put up the decorations at the tavern and I had been busy shopping for gifts. Janey knew to go to Cynthia's after school, and I would pick her up when I was done with my errands.

"Why can't you wait and take me with you?" Janey had asked that morning.

"Because, I'm going Christmas shopping," I said.

"Oh," she said, and giggled. "For me, yeah, for me!"

Well, that was the truth and by the time six in the evening rolled around I thought I had done a good day's work. So I headed home, stopping at Cynthia's to pick up Janey. Bradley was working late and the two of them had just concocted dinner, so I ate with them. Afterwards, Janey went inside to watch television, leaving me a moment alone with Cynthia.

"Everything okay with Janey today?"

"Sure, why wouldn't it be?"

"Well, we've had a couple difficult nights, that's all. This coming holiday season, Cyn, I'm just worried about her. She and Annie shared so much, I don't think I can possibly live up to her Christmas memories. And as much fun as I had today buying her gifts, they're just trinkets. The real spirit of the holiday may just evade us."

"Oh, that's where I think you're wrong," said Cynthia. She shushed me while she peeked around the corner. Janey was preoccupied watching the lighting of the Rockefeller Center Christmas Tree. "All day long, Janey kept asking me what gift she could get you for Christmas. Something special, she said—her words. She was quite insistent; we spent so much time in the card store, looking at ornaments and such. Oops, I promised Janey I wouldn't spoil the surprise, not that I've given anything away." She patted my arm. "Brian, you've done a remarkable job with Janey these past few months, and she knows it. So don't worry about Christmas. Just keep doing what you've been doing; that's the best gift of all."

So Janey had been looking at tree ornaments. For a second I contemplated telling Cynthia my fears about my missing ornament and then thought better of it. Explaining the situation would require explaining its significance and I wasn't prepared to get into that involved story, not now.

So instead the three of us watched the remainder of the Christmas special together, Janey clapping at the ice skaters, and once the big tree at 30 Rock had been lit, I gathered her into my arms and we left Cynthia's warm home. On the quick ride back to the farmhouse Janey kept stealing looks into the empty back seat. Puzzlement covered her face.

"You were gone a long time, Brian—where are the packages?"

"In the trunk, silly," I said. "I see I'm going to have to find a good hiding place, so you don't accidentally on purpose uncover them before Christmas."

"Brian you can't do something accidentally on purpose."

"Oh, I think you could," I said, which made her giggle.

I left the packages in the trunk and joined Janey inside. It was already past nine, so I told her to get ready for bed. A few minutes later I went upstairs, found her already tucked in bed and reading a book. I sat on the bed's edge, smoothing her hair out of her eyes.

"How can you read with your hair covering your eyes."

"It's not a very good book," she said.

"So why not read something else?"

"Because, Brian, I started this book and I have to finish it. Because that's what you do, you finish what you started."

It was good advice.

"Well, don't read for too long, tomorrow's a school day."

As I readied to leave a few minutes later Janey said, "I know where you can hide my gifts."

"Where is that?"

"Inside the windmill. That's what Momma used to do, every year. She would tell me the windmill was off-limits from Thanksgiving to Christmas. 'You never know what kind of project I'm working on, Janey.' That's what she would tell me; I remember, because even if I sledded down the hill and got too close to the windmill she would remind me of our deal. So go ahead if you want, Brian, it's another tradition."

"It certainly is, thanks, Janey."

I kissed her goodnight, shut off the light and then wandered downstairs. As I fixed myself a cup of tea, I thought of Janey's suggestion. Wondered if maybe it was less a suggestion and more a passive aggressive command on her part. Whichever, I decided that's what I would do. I checked on Janey, who was sound asleep, and then feeling like I could spare a quick fifteen minutes, I went outside into the cold night, gathered up the three large packages and carried them from the driveway and through the field to the windmill. The sails were silent on this calm evening. I opened the door and set the bags down on the ground floor. Should I just leave them here in the corner, or was there a better hiding place? Then I remembered that upstairs in Annie's art studio was a closet. So I wound my way up the circular staircase, the bags bulky in my arms. But eventually I stuffed them into the closet, closing the door with just enough room to spare. Then I impulsively sat down on Annie's stool.

Not much had changed inside the studio. Annie's easel was still set-up, though no canvas sat upon it. Her paints were laid out, capped against the air. Brushes occupied a jelly jar on the shelf. Surrounded by the tools that had helped reveal Annie's heart, I was suddenly enveloped by her presence. This room was special, as it was the first place Annie and I had made love, truly where we had poured out our troubles, where we had bonded over mutual sorrow, mutual betrayal, and later, mutual healing. In this room we had tried to forge a future.

Common sense told me I should return to the farmhouse, but I was caught up in the moment, feeling Annie's spirit seep beneath my skin. I didn't want to let go; so little time had passed since she'd left us but in other ways it had seemed an eternity. Being responsible for Janey, it was by far the most demanding role of my life, and also the most rewarding. I had wished for Annie and I and Janey to be one and instead I'd had to settle for the knowledge that not all wishes are granted. My desires, though, meant nothing, because everything was about Janey.

Wiping away a tear that had crept out of my eye, I stood from Annie's stool, walked to the cabinet where she had stored her paintings. She had loved to paint the windmill, and had even given me one of them. As I flipped through several of the canvases, I smiled at the memory of first seeing these wonderful landscapes. How shy Annie had been, how modest she'd been of her talent. Before I realized it, I had settled onto the floor and was going through each of the drawers, coming upon many paintings, sketches and pencil drawings that I had never before seen. I had never felt the need or the want before, sensing that I was going where I wasn't welcome. These represented Annie's past, her life before I had accidentally (on purpose?) stumbled into it. One painting in particular caused my heart to skip a beat and that tear that I wiped away earlier, it returned and this time it brought with it others.

In the bottom drawer was a family portrait, Annie and her husband Dan, and in the middle of them was Janey as an infant, probably no more than three months old. Just as I had discovered in the attic last week, here now was further proof of the daunting task before me. Janey had once belonged to a loving family, a whole family, and circumstances, maybe destiny, had taken that from her, leaving her alone in the world, except for me. Was I constantly to be haunted by these memories, by all that Janey had lost? The past was a place you couldn't avoid, the littlest thing able to spark them back to life. Like a painting, a ceramic windmill, even a shiny glass ornament. How was I supposed to respond to them? Hide them from her as a way of protecting her? Or was I just protecting myself, avoiding the pain? History claimed me as an expert at avoiding issues.

That's what I did, at least for now. I returned the portrait to the drawer, closed it and then closed off the windmill, too, locking the door behind me as I retreated back up the hill. Once I returned to the farmhouse, a surprising sight awaited me. Janey was sitting on the stairs, clutching at her stuffed purple frog.

"Hey, Janey, what's wrong?"

"You weren't here."

"Oh, honey, I'm sorry," I said, immediately going to her side. "I went to put away the gifts and wasn't planning on being gone long. I guess time got away from me. But, Janey, you were sound asleep—and you never wake up once that happens."

She nodded her head slowly. "I know, but, well, I felt bad, Brian, that's why I couldn't sleep. I keep telling you these things, you know, ways Momma and I celebrated Christmas. But maybe you have your own ways of doing things. You don't have to hide the gifts in the windmill and you don't have to chop down a tree for me, it's okay."

"No, no, Janey, I want to do what makes you happy. I enjoy learning about your Christmas traditions," I said, my mind blown by what she was saying. Here I was, letting slip my responsibilities by getting lost in the past, and she was apologizing to me. I hugged her tight, trying to figure out a way I could take back my mistake. And then an idea came to me. "I'll tell you what, Janey, if it will make you feel better, how about I show you some of my holiday traditions."

"Like what?"

"Well, remember that big tree in New York we just saw being lit on the television?"

"Yes?"

"How would you like to see it for real?"

"That big tree, really?"

"It's where I used to live—New York City. I saw it every year I lived there," I said. "So what do you say?"

She didn't answer immediately, but then said, "Can we go ice skating?"

"Janey Sullivan, we can do anything you want to do," I said, silently adding that I would do anything for her. No matter what.

CHAPTER FIVE

"Janey, let's go, we've got to get going," I said, running up the stairs to her room. I had my coat on and my car keys dangling from my fingers. Our latest adventure was upon us, and where was Janey? Not in her room, it appeared. Still, I nosed around, wondering if she was playing a game of hide and seek with me. In a way, she was. Because as I got down on my knees to peek beneath the bed, a surprise awaited me. Not Janey, who she was still unaccounted for. What I found instead was the little box that contained my family Christmas ornament. All this time wondering what had happened to it, and here it was stashed under Janey's bed. Why would she do such a thing? A wave of emotion washed over me as I grabbed for the box. The sound of footsteps caused me to pull back and I returned to my feet just as Janey entered her room.

"Hey, where were you?" I asked.

"In the attic. I was thinking about seeing that big Christmas tree, and that's when I started to feel bad because you never found that pretty ornament with your name on it. So I was looking around all those boxes—Momma sure liked to keep everything, didn't she?"

I nodded, unable to use my voice for a moment. Finally, I said, "And what did you find, Janey?"

"Nothing. Well, not the ornament. Sorry, we'll keep looking."

"Yes, we will," was my only reply.

She didn't react to that, she just said, "Okay, can we go, Brian, I'm really excited about the trip."

"Yeah, Janey, let's get out of here," I said.

"Yeah?" she scolded me.

"Oops, you got me. Sorry, yes, let's both you and I get out of here," I said.

I led her from her bedroom. Neither of us looked back and before long we were buckled into our seats and we turned out of the driveway and onto the road. It took all my concentration to follow the winding curves of Route 23. Janey happily gave a running commentary on all she saw out the window, the windmill, other cars and piles of snow and in one case, a deer standing on the edge of the woods. I said little, my mind preoccupied. Because I had found proof that Janey had lied to me.

* * *

WOW."

It never fails, pictures don't do it justice, nor does television. Nothing does but actually seeing it up close, walking amidst the streets, avenues, canyons. New York City, its magnificent skyscrapers and bustling throngs of people, the pace of a place that barely stops to catch its breath. I'd been dazzled when I first laid my eyes on it and now it was Janey's turn, and she was no less enraptured than I had been. I might have been keeping an eye on the road ahead of me, but for certain out of the corner of my other eye I stole a look at her face. Wonder gave way to awe and for the present moment the problems that existed between us melted away, hot water thrust on ice. Despite what I was feeling, there was no way I was going to ruin this trip for her.

"Wow," she repeated.

"Pretty neat, huh?" I asked.

"You lived here?" Her tone was one of incredulity, and actually at this moment I had to admit I felt similarly; had I really called this steel and glass mountain my home? That life of mine seemed so long ago, so distant, occurring before the land of the windmill had swallowed me up, lifted me out of a stark reality and into the wind-fueled fantasy of a new world.

"Yes, I guess I did."

I hadn't been back to New York since August, since before the storm that had nearly destroyed the windmill, and the feeling that washed over me now was, oddly, one of unfamiliarity. So much seemed changed, the place I'd once called home now looked foreign.

Our first stop was the Upper East Side, which I explained to Janey was where I used to live.

"That's where John lives now, right?" she asked.

"You got that right."

We had eventually done a lot of talking on the trip down. I told her about John, how he was my best friend from way back during college, my last remaining link to the city. I told her, too, how supportive John had been during my crisis earlier this year—the hepatitis that had debilitated me and the changes that had occurred at my job, the offices of the Beckford Group, both of which had precipitated my departure from the city. Last spring life had seemed about as bleak as a Dickens novel; just as lengthy, too. A distraction from wounded memories was exactly what I needed, and John would provide that with his good humor and juvenile antics.

"You'll like him," I said. "He's silly."

"You're the silly one, Brian."

"Yeah? And you like me, right?"

"That's a bad habit of yours, Brian. Momma always told me 'don't say yeah.' Remember?"

"Oops," I replied.

Janey giggled. "See? Silly."

Still, as much fun as we had on the ride down, she seemed dubious at the idea of taking a liking to this stranger who held the title of Brian's Best Friend. (My interpretation of how Janey saw certain things: all in capital letters.)

So we parked my aging Grand Am on East Eighty-Third Street, just down the block from the brick apartment building I'd once called home. Sunday afternoon and there were thankfully plenty of spots available on the block. I locked the car, grabbed hold of Janey's hand and the two of us made our way down the street.

"What are those black things—with the ladders?" she asked.

"Fire escapes."

"They look like ways robbers could break into your apartment."

"Well, there aren't any robbers around, so you don't have to worry."

We rang John's apartment, heard his voice crackling through the intercom as he buzzed us in. How many times had I taken these stairs, how many times had I not even looked around—at the scarred walls, at the dog hair that gathered in clumps in the corner of the steps, at the brightly-painted front doors of each apartment. Forest green doors against white walls. Nope, nothing had changed, yet from my new perspective as a newly-christened "country boy," the box-like living quality struck me as awfully confining.

John was standing in the doorway, all six foot two of him. He was dressed casually in jeans and a sweater, not unlike Janey and myself. All of us appeared ready for a day of adventure. I took care of introductions, with John bending down so he was at eye level with Janey.

"Brian said you were cute," John said. "He was so wrong."

Janey tossed me a skeptical glance, as though to say, "Is he for real?" I gave John a look that said, "Get out of this one."

But John, smoothie that he is, masterfully recovered. "Because you're far too grown up to be called cute. That's for babies and infants. You're very, very pretty, Janey. I like your freckles."

Janey blushed at John's compliment and I laughed at his surprising level of charm. Then I edged passed him with a knowing look, saying I wanted to see what he'd done to destroy my place.

"Your place? I don't see any cows around here."

That made Janey laugh and suddenly it was like the two of them had been friends for years, poking fun of me the link between them. John gave us the full tour—the bedroom, the kitchen, the living room, three rooms in one, with barely a decoration on the walls. He once adorned them with posters of rock groups and movies, but he seemed to be in a transitional stage. One thing I did notice, set atop his dresser, was the postcard of the windmill I had sent months ago; nice to know there was a sentimental bone amidst his cynical nature. The tour took all of one minute, with Janey asking, "Where's the rest of your house?"

John assumed it was a rhetorical question. So he grabbed his coat and escorted us out of his home. As we walked to the corner to summon a cab, I asked after "the love of his life."

"Anna's meeting us at 30 Rock."

I took a step backward as my smile deflated. "Her name is Anna?"

"Yeah, why, what's the big deal?"

"Nothing, John, sorry," I said, a fearful chill running down my spine. "It's just, well, for a second all I could think about was Annie. Guess the similarity in names took me by surprise."

"Oh man, it didn't even register, sorry," he said. "She going be okay with that?"

I looked down at Janey, to find her looking square up at me.

"What are you two talking about way up there?"

She either hadn't heard the woman's name or it hadn't made any impact on her. Regardless, the subject was dropped as a cab stopped at the corner of Eighty-Third and Second Avenue, and we hopped in, John giving the cabbie instructions to get us to Rockefeller Center. Janey had been curious to ride in a cab and now that we were inside one, she watched with dubious caution as the driver began to weave his way through traffic.

"When do you pay?" Janey asked, leaning in close to me so the driver couldn't hear.

"When our trip is over."

She seemed to accept this, but still, she kept glancing over at the meter as the fare clicked higher and higher.

Fifteen minutes slipped by as we waded our way down Fifth Avenue. We got out at Forty-Ninth Street, Janey watching as John paid the driver and a young couple took possession of what had been our cab, now theirs. It quickly dashed down the avenue, and we went in search of the tree at Rockefeller Center. Given its size, it wasn't difficult to find.

There was no other place like Manhattan for the holidays. The storefronts were extensively and, in some cases, excessively decorated, big red ribbons hung on the side of buildings, a large wreath with gold and silver balls was suspended over the intersection at Fifty-Seventh Street and Fifth, its lights visible even in the daylight. Janey guessed that it sparkled at night. At last we turned the corner and the giant tree came into view. Standing nearly one hundred feet into the air, obsessively covered with colorful lights, there was no denying its power, the hold it had over the assembled crowd of people. Probably thousands of visitors had chosen this moment to visit the tree, itself more than a tradition but an institution for the city of New York, the ideal symbol for the season. Janey grabbed my hand and pulled me closer, to where we virtually stood beneath the great pine branches. She craned her neck, trying to look all the way up.

"Wow," she said, a word that would go over-used this day.

Especially when she took a moment's break from staring at the tree to meet John's girlfriend, who had just showed up.

"Wow," Janey said again, and this time, well, I have to admit I thought the same thing.

Her name was Anna Santorini, a nice Brooklyn-born Italian girl who was probably the dictionary definition of beautiful. She was five foot six, had large brown eyes and short black hair that was flawlessly styled. Her lips were lightly coated with red lipstick. With her black coat and red scarf to match, colors that perfectly complemented her skin tone, she had caught more than our eyes. Envious men all over watched as John gave her a welcoming kiss on the lips.

Then he took care of the introductions.

"Wow," Janey repeated. "You're beautiful."

"Thank you, Janey, what a very sweet thing to say. And quite the compliment, coming from such a beauty herself."

Well, that did it. Janey dropped my hand and took hold of Anna's and for the rest of the day they would be inseparable. Maybe it was having a mother figure around. She was someone whom Janey could talk to; a nice change of pace from good old reliable Brian Duncan, who knew as much about little girls and as he did about farming. (Despite John's frequent claims.) In any case, the two ladies walked ahead of us while exploring Rockefeller Center, watching the ice skaters below us, then as we wandered across the street to the windows at Saks. Their new bond gave John and me a chance to reconnect. We talked nonsense really, though I did give my seal of approval to Anna. John positively beamed when I mentioned Anna, which made me wonder, had Peter Pan found an outbound flight from Neverland? Shame, I used to enjoy my visits there.

Janey tugged at my sleeve, stirring me from my reverie.

"Come on, Brian, let's go inside this store," she said, pointing to the entrance to Saks.

I laughed. "Aren't you a bit young for diamonds?"

"No, I bet they have nice Christmas ornaments, maybe you can get a new one, you know, in place of the one that's missing."

From this magical land I was transported back to reality, to the knowledge that Janey had taken the ornament and for whatever reason continued to lie about it. And here she was, suggesting we replace something that was irreplaceable. A shadow darkened my face as I realized I hadn't actually seen the actual ornament; just the box it was stored in. Why was she so insistent that I get a new one? A horrible thought occurred, one I dismissed right there and then. There had to be some other rational explanation. It couldn't have broken.

"What ornament?" Anna asked.

"Oh, it's nothing," I said, wishing to downplay it.

But John, who had known me the longest, knew its significance. "The one from Philip?"

"Later, John," I said, and for once he actually listened to me.

We didn't go into the store, and instead we resumed our walk and gradually the terrible images that had flashed through my mind gave way to warmer memories of the life I'd had in New York. It had changed, just as I had, as Janey had. Lost in my world of Linden Corners, it was clear that the world that was New York still turned, life went on, and I had to wonder if maybe I missed it.

* * *

We were headed for lunch at a Mexican place near Times Square. I directed everyone down Forty-Seventh Street, wanting to at least walk by a store that held good memories for me. Eli's Jeweler's, the sign read. I peeked inside, saw the little man busily attending to a happy couple. I smiled, glad that Eli was still in the business of selling dreams. As I was about to leave, Eli looked up and for the briefest of moments our eyes locked. I raised my index finger and spun it through the air, a handmade windmill. He nodded once before returning to his customers and I returned to my friends. It was Eli who had introduced me to the concept of tilting at windmills, though how prophetic his words had been only I knew.

On Forty-Third Street, we got settled at our table and placed lunch orders. In time, drinks were before us—wine for John and Anna, iced tea for me, hot cocoa for Janey.

"What, you're still not drinking? Thought the doc gave you the a-okay?" John said to me as I sipped my iced tea.

"Yeah, well, I've got responsibilities. Who needs it?"

"Brian, you own a bar."

"I run a bar. Very different from going to one."

"Semantics," he said.

I apologized to Anna. "Sorry, old news."

She informed me that John had given her a full debriefing of my new life and how it had come about. She asked after the windmill and suddenly Janey jumped into the conversation, relating how the story of how the Van Diver family had come to build the windmill out of necessity, how the Sullivan family had inherited the old farm and done their best to restore the great old mill. I was surprised at the depth of knowledge Janey had, marveled too by her sense of storytelling. For an eight-year-old, there was lots of raw talent. Who knew? Maybe we had a writer in our midst. Janey, though, was particularly modest when I complimented her skills.

"You really have to see the windmill yourself," she told them.

"Yes, I've only seen the postcard," Anna said.

"Oh, you've been to John's place?" I asked.

John shot me a look, but Anna just laughed it off. "Several times, Brian."

"Wow, I never thought I'd see the day John Oliver was embarrassed about having a woman over to his place."

"Hey, Bri, there's a kid present," John stated.

That produced further laughter, even from Janey who thankfully didn't understand why we were laughing. I was having a great time, and I was glad that Janey had been willing to make this trip. I loved my life in Linden Corners, don't get me wrong, but once in awhile the open road called to me, that sense of wanderlust that had first captured me nearly a year ago. Or maybe my former life wanted me back, the things I missed, this city and its energy. As much as Linden Corners was a morning kind of town, New York was just the opposite, gaining strength with each passing hour of the day until the sun was down and the neon was lit. The switch in lifestyle was a literal experiment in night and day for me.

Speaking of switches, the conversation took a major one.

"So Maddie left town," John informed with me with his customary lack of grace.

"Who's Maddie?" Janey asked.

There was silence at our little table for four.

"What, are we not allowed to talk about her? Come on, Brian, that's water over the bridge, I thought."

"I know all about what's going on with Maddie," I said. "She's living in Seattle, she's happy, she's moved on.

Got a job with Microsoft and is making a mint. Just like she always wanted."

"That's not all she ever wanted."

"John, there's a reason why they call it the past."

"Okay, I'm sorry. I just wasn't sure, you know, if you were...over her."

"Who's Maddie? And why do you need to be over her, Brian?" Janey asked again.

Anna said, "She's just someone Brian used to know, it's not important now. Say, why don't you and I go pick out a couple songs on the jukebox, Janey? Maybe something with a good beat, maybe we'll get Brian dancing. Does your Dad dance?"

Again, there was awkward silence at the table—another sensitive topic breached, but there was no way Anna could have known that Janey never used the word "Dad" concerning me. But before I had a chance to explain, Janey simply said, "Not very well."

Then they went off to make their musical selections. Me, I selected John as my target and hit him on the arm, hard.

"I guess I deserve that—for bringing up Maddie," he said, his version of apologizing. He'd always been sensitive to her side of what had happened, he'd always had a soft spot for her. Maddie Chasen had fallen victim to corporate ambitions, had let it get the best of her, it could happen to anyone. Anyone, that is, with the drive to get to the top and the willingness to betray anyone to get there.

"You okay, though, you know, about that dad stuff?"

"Janey handled it very well. Better than I might have."

"I take it something like that has happened before? Can't be an easy thing to deal with, the poor kid. Makes me realize exactly what you've taken on with agreeing to raise her. And don't get me wrong, Brian, Janey's great and from what I can see, she's nuts about you. Is that enough, though, to get through, uh…this? I know it sucked what happened this fall. But you know, I keep thinking that maybe if you and Maddie had worked things out, maybe the two of you—and Janey? Hey, maybe it's not too late, since the punk Justin Warfiend—uh, Warfield, and that dumb stunt from the spring is long over. That's the thing about the past, you can leave it there, but people have to move forward, they make futures. Imagine it, Bri, you and Maddie and Janey?"

"I wouldn't do that to Annie's memory," I said rather forcefully. "Maddie is...Maddie's in a different time zone; hell, John, a different life zone. Let's leave it at that, okay? Enough couch-talk today, I'm fine, Janey's great and we've got a great thing going. Let's talk about you instead—specifically, you and Anna. She's great."

"That she is, my friend, she's changed my life. Women, they can do that, in an instant."

Finally John was talking my language.

"Uh, can I ask you about something else?" John said.

"Something other than Maddie? I'd welcome it."

"You okay, you know, money-wise? And before you get yourself in a snit, I'm asking because I'm worried. Look at you, Brian. You're taking care of this little girl—and from what I can see, doing a great job. But that's a lot to take on; Janey's gonna need more than just your love, she's going to need security. And I mean financial security. Now, this is probably nothing that you haven't thought of, but, hey, can the two of you really survive on a bartender's salary? Especially considering you've had to hire part-time help so you can spend more time with her. You had your savings, but your six-month sabbatical from the world took care of a lot of that. So, I guess I'm asking, is everything being met? You know, end to end?"

As much as I didn't wish to discuss this with John, I knew he meant well. Just as he did when he'd mentioned Maddie. So I reassured him that everything was fine.

"At Thanksgiving, my father actually handed me a check for twenty-five thousand dollars. It's his way of endorsing the changes I've made to my life plan. That ought to help for awhile."

"Yeah, but did you endorse the check?"

That was the danger of best friends. They knew you too well.

"Everything's fine," I said, non-committingly.

"Okay, good, I just wanted to make sure."

Of course I didn't tell John that the check still was hidden away in a desk drawer back at the farmhouse.

As he took a sip of his wine, he assured me the serious portion of the day was over.

"At last," I remarked.

Our food arrived and the four of us settled in for a grand old Mexican feast, quesadillas and burritos and rice with beans, the kind of meal that was scarce in the meatloaf and potatoes menu that Linden Corners subsisted on. There was lots more chatter, John and I dominating the conversation but only because we had so much history, so much to catch up on and to share with these new people in our lives.

Afterwards, we grabbed another cab that took us up to Central Park. From there, we ventured to Wollman Rink. The four of us rented skates and took to the ice. I had never been very agile when it came to skating, but Anna was a natural and Janey was a fast learner and soon the two of them were whizzing by me and John, laughing and smiling the whole time, no doubt at our expense.

A while later John and I gave up and we just hung out by the railing, talking. And though we talked often on the telephone, there was nothing like face to face contact, the conversation flowing much more naturally, the shifts from topic to topic less obvious. Luckily he said nothing more about Maddie; we talked mostly about holiday plans. John wasn't going home, instead was headed to Anna's family for a traditional Christmas Eve feast.

"What about you? You bringing Janey to your parents?"

So I told him about my parents' plan to take a cruise. "New beginnings in the Duncan household."

"You okay with that?"

"I'm thirty-four, John, I've spent more Christmases than I ever thought I would have with my parents. I think Philip would understand. The tradition, it lives, just in another form." He let the subject go, and I told him then about the annual party at the tavern, and suggested he might want to stop by.

"Stop by? Brian, your little fantasy town in three hours away."

"So, stay overnight at the farmhouse," I said. "You and Anna."

"You gonna wake me in the morning to milk cows?"

"Hey John?"

"Yeah?"

"You're such a jerk."

As the day wound down, we walked back to the Upper East Side because it was not too far from the skating rink. The beautiful day we'd been blessed with had turned noticeably cooler and I made sure Janey was nicely bundled up. I was proud of her today, her resourcefulness, her willingness to try new things and to meet new people. As worried as I had been about once again taking her from the known comforts of Linden Corners, I think with John and Anna we had given her an experience she wouldn't soon forget. The magical world that is Christmas in New York.

Magic had a way of disappearing in a poof of smoke. Because soon I would return to Linden Corners and to the troubles that I'd left back there, hidden beneath the bed and maybe in Janey's heart as well. Troubles that only I seemed to be carrying; Janey was too lost in this special day to remember the deceit that plagued us.

* * *

Night had fallen and we were exhausted from an excursion that had seemed to take us all over the varied neighborhoods of Manhattan. It was in front of John's apartment building that we said our good-byes with hugs and handshakes, good wishes for a happy holiday. Then, as Janey and I made our way down the street, she turned back just in time to see Anna and John locked in a tight embrace, kissing like teenagers. I watched Janey's wide-eyed expression, wondering just what she was thinking. When the two lovebirds finally broke apart, they saw Janey gazing up at them.

"You forget something?" John asked.

Janey shook her head. "I just wanted to remind you, you know, to come and see the windmill," she said. "You'd be very welcome."

We left them with big smiles on their faces, hopped into the car and sped away from the city, fortunately going against traffic. The smile on my face didn't seem to want to dissipate either, not until a half hour into our trip when Janey, who'd been quiet and obviously mulling over something in her complicated little brain, blurted out, "You never answered the question, Brian."

"Which one was that?"

"About that woman named Maddie. Was she your girlfriend when you lived here?"

"Yes, Janey she was."

She was silent a moment, a stubborn sponge, taking awhile to absorb that information. Then she asked, "Were you going to marry her?"

"What makes you ask that?"

"Well, at Thanksgiving, your sister talked about that woman Lucy, and she said you wanted to marry her. And you told me that you were going to marry my momma. So, I just wondered..." She hesitated, which was unlike her. Janey was the type to just attack a problem head on, she just let things out. And then she did, as she asked, "Did you also want to marry Maddie?"

I thought about Maddie Chasen, her platinum blonde hair, the way her voice would slip into its natural Southern tones when she got mad. I thought about that wonderful afternoon last year when we had strolled down Forty-Seventh Street—the Diamond District—and how we had cooed together over a ring that absolutely sparkled. How the next day I had purchased it, and how circumstances had brought me to return it without ever having presented her with it. But on that return visit, good old Eli the Jeweler, he had had words of advice for me. All of us, he said, must tilt at windmills. And I had, literally and figuratively, as those words had taken me straight into Linden Corners, straight into the reticent, but ultimately welcoming arms of Annie Sullivan. Had I wanted to marry Maddie? Yeah, that had been my plan. But that had not been life's plan. And as much as I understood this, I reflected that Janey wouldn't understand the grays in life; answers to her came in black and white, yes and no.

"I suppose so, Janey," I said, "that yes, at one time in my life I did want to marry Maddie."

"Before you met Momma?"

"Yeah," I said, my voice barely above a whisper in the darkness of the car. Outside only the headlights guided our way home. Janey didn't bother to correct my grammar this time, she merely quieted down again, her face scrunched up again in thought. This adventure had yielded such deep discussions, and that was good because I wanted to encourage Janey to ask questions when she was curious. The reason for these trips, both to Philadelphia and to New York, was for Janey to get to know a bit about me, to know where I had come from and why her being in my life meant so much for me. And maybe if she began to feel closer to me, she wouldn't pull the stunt she had with the ornament.

"Brian?"

"Yes, Janey?" I replied, concentrating on the traffic up ahead.

"Why wasn't your brother Philip at your family's Thanksgiving? You showed me his picture up on the wall, remember?"

I felt adrenaline rush through me and had my foot been more firmly on the accelerator we might have crashed into the car ahead of us. Instead, we stopped short. In the silence of the car, Janey looking up expectantly with her curious, earnest eyes, I said, my voice a near whisper, "Philip was sick, Janey, and...and he can no longer be with us. Philip…he died."

INTERLUDE

That night, as young girl and guardian slept peacefully within the farmhouse, outside the wind had picked up, blowing across the open field, bringing to life the windmill's mighty sails. Gently they turned, then with more drive and energy, more passion. And as those sails spun in the lonely night, a sound carried over the waves of the wind, a persistent whistle that awakened the little girl from her deep sleep. Though she didn't know what it was—who it was—still, she could undoubtedly feel a presence trying to reach out to her. She'd been dreaming of Christmas, of the gifts stored away until the morning of the 25th.

She threw back the warm blankets and dropped her bare feet to the floor. For a moment she listened for the sound of activity and when she was satisfied that he was sleeping, she grabbed her robe and cinched it around her waist. She opened the door to her room, padded her way down the hallway. His own door was closed, but she knew he slept lightly, unlike herself who enjoyed drifting deep into delicious dreams. In fact, she couldn't be certain what had awakened her at such an hour. Still, she felt the need to venture downstairs, where she put boots on her feet, a jacket over her robe and thick mittens on her hands. A finishing touch of a hat and she was ready for the outdoors. In the mirror that hung in the hallway, she saw her reflection and for a second she quietly giggled; she looked ridiculous in this winterized pajama get-up.

Once outside, she gazed high into the night sky. A brilliant half moon lit the sky, little sparkles of stars lighting her way. Through the snowy field she traveled, until she came upon the windmill's lone, majestic presence. Backlit by the moon, it was like the sails were encased in their own glow, a sharp contrast to the black backdrop of night. She'd never been outside at this hour before and she knew it was wrong, but tonight that didn't matter. And even though she imagined she should be afraid, she didn't let her fear stop her. Of course, the door that led inside the windmill was locked, he had seen to it ever since deciding to hide the gifts here. To uncover them, that wasn't the reason behind her journey.

The two of them had only been back from their New York adventure a night, and all day at school she had talked Ashley's ear off, describing the wonderful images of the holiday season she had witnessed. She also told her friend about Brian's other life—"He was smiling all day, Ashley, like he missed his old home." "Do you think he'll move back one day? With all his stupid things, his ornament and everything," her friend countered with, and that had set her mind reeling. What if Brian tired of her? Before going to bed that night, she had sent a wish out upon the wind, hoping it would find her mother somewhere in her otherworldly travels. The wind always knew, because it circled the world and found every destination, even those hidden from the people who still live.

Now Janey was certain that with the wind's rattling against her window tonight, that a reply had come.

She was getting cold and wanted to find a way inside the windmill. Then she remembered the spare key, and she reached down on the ground. A small crack in the structure had been the perfect hiding place for a key and lucky for her, it remained there. Almost like it was meant to be. And so Janey unlocked the door and she made her way inside. But inside the windmill it was dark, and she had to wait a moment until her eyes fully adjusted to the lack of light. Then she circled her up way to the second level and went into her momma's studio. From there she peeked out the small window, realized her journey wasn't yet complete. From the second floor, another door opened to the catwalk that encircled the windmill. It was here Janey went, where she could see the sails pass right before her eyes, where she knew her momma had loved to watch the world pass her by.

She collected her thoughts before speaking. She thought about Brian, of the very first time she saw him right here, at the base of the windmill. Like he had appeared out of nowhere, something born out of her wishes. But now, she was getting to know the real-life Brian Duncan, and she realized there was a lot more to learn.

"I'm glad you called, Momma," Janey said, speaking into the wind. "Brian's been real good to me, just like you said he would. He took me on a trip, actually two of them, and I met people he knows. Momma? Did Brian really want to marry you? I think so, because he's always wanting to get married. There was Lucy and then some lady named Maddie. Did you know about her? Brian says Maddie came to the windmill once but I don't really remember. I don't want Brian to get married, because then I'll have a new mom, even though Brian's not even my real dad. People keep calling him that. I overheard him talking with Cynthia—all he wants is for me to be happy. He's worried about Christmas. Me, too, because I don't know what gift to get him. He has this beautiful ornament that he's going to hang on the tree. Except it's missing. Can you help me? That's all I ask. Because I thought I knew who Brian was, and now, wow, there's so much more to know. Momma, he has a sister who's not very nice and he had a brother, but he died."

The wind blew past, the sails turned.

"Momma, I think I did something bad, and now maybe Brian doesn't want to take care of me anymore. He took me to New York and showed me places he used to live and work and I met a friend of his. I had fun, but I think he had more fun. He's been very quiet since we got back from our trip. So that's why I think he misses his old life. Do you think so too? I'll wait to hear from you."

So she watched the sails turn in anticipation of some kind of response, not unlike the time before Thanksgiving when Brian had visited. If she listened hard enough, maybe an answer could be heard. Until then, she had to be contented.

"Thanks for listening, Momma, I love you and I miss you."

She felt better just saying the words. She felt warmer, too, even out in this bitter cold. As though her momma was feeding her strength, instilling within her an inner glow that could battle any temperature, challenge any crisis.

"Oh, and Merry Christmas, Momma."

Janey returned to the farmhouse, where she noted on the kitchen clock it was three forty-seven in the morning. Brian was still sleeping, and in seconds so would she be, clutching at her stuffed purple frog. A large smile would cover her face as she slept, maybe from an idea coming to her, one that could help make Christmas special for Brian.

The next morning, she found Brian making breakfast in the kitchen.

"How did you sleep, sweetie?" he asked.

"Okay. I had a very weird dream."

Weird, she said, because she had to wonder what her winter boots were doing beside her bed, still wet with the remnants of snow.

PART TWO

New Traditions

CHAPTER SIX

While having noticeable drawbacks, living in denial was not without its appeal. I had not confronted Janey about the missing ornament, feeling that once we opened that can of worms little good could come of it. We would upset the delicate balance we'd achieved. With all she had been through this year, with our relationship unsteady and changing daily, confronting her seemed the wrong approach. Also, I suppose I was waiting for her to broach the subject, and so far she hadn't seen fit to. And so I allowed our busy lives to progress without interruption, telling myself it was just a silly ornament and her needs were most important, all the while ignoring the big issue; one of trust.

So instead, we had other matters filling our days and nights. In Linden Corners, there always seemed to be some event to look forward to. Since my arrival in town, I had shared with the residents a joyous Memorial Day and been welcomed by George Connors' summer tradition he called First Friday. Myself, I had created a companion celebration, Second Saturday, at the tavern in honor of George and just this past fall the villagers had come together to remember Annie in the most remarkable way possible, a coming together of community that helped restore the windmill. So now it was with eagerness that I and my newfound friends were looking forward to the Christmas Party at George's Tavern, which we would hold the night before Christmas Eve. I had been industrious in sending out personal invitations, and had also posted several flyers around town; at the bank and at the Five-O, as well as at the tavern itself.

As for Christmas, it was still more than a week away, though at the farmhouse it might as well have been two months off for all the decorations that abounded. Janey hadn't pressured me much either, not about the lights or the tree or anything. In truth, we hadn't been spending as much quality time together since the New York trip. She filled her hours playing with her friends and helping to plan the school holiday party, helping Cynthia, too, who had her own annual tradition of bottling jars filled with jellies and jams. So, knowing that Janey and I needed to solidify our holiday plans, it was with new resolve that I awoke that Saturday morning. I was certain that by day's end we would have a tree and our first holiday together would be under way.

At eight that morning I knocked on Janey's door, heard no reply and when I opened it, saw that she was already up. I made my way downstairs and found her in front of the television; she was watching Dora the Explorer and laughing at the colorful antics.

"Morning," I said.

"Hi, Brian," she replied, not even looking away from the screen.

"You want breakfast? It's Saturday; what about pancakes?"

"I had cereal," she said, pointing to her empty bowl.

"Oh, uh, okay."

I stood in the living room for a moment, feeling at a loss for words and hoping Janey might fill the empty void. She didn't and eventually I went into the kitchen, made coffee and pondered why I was getting the brush off. Could she be reading my thoughts, could she know what I knew about the box beneath her bed? What I realized was now wasn't the moment to announce my plan for the day, chopping down our first Christmas tree. Deciding to tell her later, I showered and shaved and took care of some of the household duties I'd been neglecting. Some vacuuming, some much needed laundry, all of which kept me busy while Janey contented herself with mindless cartoons. Around eleven o'clock Janey popped her head into the laundry room and asked if I could give her a ride to Ashley's house.

"We're going to make cookies—Christmas cookies," she said. "Her parents promised we could."

"It's not on the calendar—when did you make these plans?"

"Oh, earlier."

"Earlier when?"

"What difference does it makes, Brian? I want to go over to Ashley's—she's waiting for me."

"Well, she's going to have to wait longer. We've got plans today."

"We do?"

"We're going with Gerta to get the tree. We talked about this—earlier."

She didn't appreciate my throwing her own ideas back in her face. "Oh, well, you don't really need me for that," she replied, then informed me that she was going to pack her bag, she was probably staying overnight at Ashley's. She turned away from me then and I almost called out to her. But I decided to let this incident pass—for the moment. Her attitude, her tone, had shocked me and I needed time not only to absorb it but to calm down. Had this exchange actually happened?

I let an hour pass by; she didn't come to me again about a ride to her friend's house. Then, as I brought clean laundry to her room, I asked her to join me. With reluctance, she finally came up the stairs and sat on her bed, her arms crossed. She couldn't look at me.

"What?" she said.

"I don't know what that was all about before and I'm going to choose to ignore it. But what I'm not going to put up with is you not being there for the cutting down of the tree. You told me a couple weeks ago that you wanted to get the tree, just like you and your momma did. It's a special memory, Janey, one I want to share with you. So I'll make you a deal, you join me and Gerta, then you can go to Ashley's later. But no sleepover, not tonight."

She said nothing. But in doing so, she spoke volumes. She wasn't happy being told what to do and I wasn't happy having to be firm with her. This was uncharted territory for us; sure she had been unusually distant with me a couple weeks ago but we'd gotten through that after the day of sledding. Now, suddenly, the tension between us was back and stronger than before; Janey was acting uncharacteristically defiant.

"Do we have a deal? Janey? Think about it, imagine when Christmas comes around and we don't have a tree decorated."

She gazed up at me, worry spreading across those freckled features of hers. For the briefest of moments, as no doubt visions of an empty Christmas morning filled her mind, I saw the Janey I knew, the Janey who had stolen my heart. Who knows, maybe the day's adventure would cure her of whatever was bothering her.

She asked tentatively, "Can I pick out the tree?"

"Can you pick out the tree? What, you think you're just along for the ride? Your presence is vital. I've never picked out a tree before. I need your expertise."

"Then okay," she said.

The barest hint of a smile had emerged, and I felt myself breathe easier.

Before I left the room, I kneeled down beside her and gently took hold of her hands. She gazed right into my eyes. Her own were wet.

"You know, Janey, if something's bothering you, you can tell me about it," I said. "You can tell me anything. Okay?"

She nodded, but said nothing.

I kissed the top of her head and then went to call Gerta.

* * *

Green's Tree Farm was fifteen miles away, just up Route 22 north. Janey and I had stopped first to pick up Gerta Connors, as she too was in need of a tree for the holidays and I had agreed to help her chop it down. In the back of the truck I had packed an ax, as well as a saw. I'd never fetched my own Christmas tree before, so I wasn't sure exactly what tool would work best. In Manhattan, every deli on every corner sold high-priced trees, creating a traffic bottleneck for pedestrians the whole month long. So this adventure had all the makings of something new and fresh; not unlike the tree we would end up with.

Janey, too, seemed to come around. As though the cloud she'd been under had passed, sunshine returned to her sweet face. Up in the sky, however, thick clouds hovered and the snow had begun to fall just as we pulled into Green's parking lot.

"Glad I wore my warm boots," Gerta said. "Will you hold my arm, Janey, while we go hiking up that mountain?"

"Sure," Janey said.

Albert Green Sr., the proprietor of the tree farm that had been in business for three decades, greeted us personally, handing out a brochure that described the various types of trees we would find on our trek.

"Let me know which one you get, I'll give you top-notch instructions for caring for it," he said, his weathered face cracked with a smile. "Heck, you'll be able to keep it till Memorial Day, ha ha."

"Why would we want to keep a tree in the house for that long?" Janey asked him.

We all laughed at her innocent comment, though based on her scrunched up nose I could tell she'd been serious. Still, it instilled in us the right mood in which to launch our journey, one that would take longer than I expected. Trying to please a little girl by choosing the perfect tree for Christmas, well, that wasn't as easy a task as I'd imagined it. Thousands of pine-scented trees surrounding us, I think Janey wanted to inspect each and every one.

Green's Tree Farm was a magnificent spread, set against the rising thrust of the majestic Berkshire Mountains; I realized we weren't far from the Massachusetts border, and who knows, the amount of time we spent walking through the cultivated, snowy paths, maybe we had already crossed into our neighboring state. Along the way we saw many other fellow tree-hunters, some of whom had been successful and were carrying their prize down the side of the mountain and back to their cars. As I trudged through the snow, the cold winter's air penetrated through my boots, I felt envious of those who were headed back toward the warmth of their cars. But Janey's infectious joy had a heat all its own and kept me going. I was glad that Janey's earlier mood had seen fit to remain back at the farmhouse. As she went running up the worn trails, pointing to tree after tree, dismissing them with the grace of a Queen before her subjects, she laughed and giggled and brought out smiles on mine and Gerta's faces.

"Oh that child," Gerta said. "So irrepressible."

No surprise, we found Gerta's tree first, since I think she was tiring too of our trip. We had to call to Janey, who was at least fifty feet ahead of us.

"Ooh, George would have loved this one," Gerta said, standing before an eight-foot, sweet-smelling Douglas Fir. "He just adored the Christmas season. He was such a good man, but the reason he liked this season? It made other men good and brought out such peace on Earth."

A picture of George Connors popped into my mind, his genial, rotund self behind the bar and welcoming me inside its cedar walls, asking what I'd like. Recovering from a case of hepatitis, I had been forbidden to drink and contended myself with an unexciting glass of seltzer. George had offered up no judgments to my order and it had been the start of a great, but far too short friendship between us. So now it was a distinct privilege to be chopping down his widow's holiday tree. A part of the Connors' family once again, not just their employee.

"Timber," I called out, feeling like a city-slicker version of Paul Bunyan. Except I had used the saw, since I had no confidence in my ability with an ax. An ax, I could injure someone—namely myself.

As the saw slid out the other side of the trunk, the great tree crashed to the ground. From behind I heard someone say, "Yeah, but if we weren't around to hear it, would it still make a sound?"

We turned around to see Mark Ravens, my relief bartender, standing before us, an ax positioned over his broad shoulder. At his side was Sara Joyner, wrapped up in a blue parka. Her face poked out from behind the fur lining. We laughed at his corny joke, shook hands all around. Janey had never met Mark before, and she smiled easily when he said it was nice to meet her finally. He charmed her that quickly. They were here to get Sara's tree, since Mark was currently living with his parents and, as he explained, "They use an artificial tree. I hate those things, the pine scent is like one of those air fresheners used in cars. Helping Sara, well, that's been fun."

"He just likes using the ax," Sara said. "A macho thing, I guess."

I tried to hide the saw.

So then we were five. Sara and Mark joined us in our search for the perfect tree, Janey explaining to them they could have the second most perfect. For the rest of our time,

Janey kept soliciting Mark's opinion on trees and when he declared one particular seven-footer to be "as perfect as perfect can be," our quest was finally over. Gerta thanked him for his good taste, as well as his speed in finding it, and we all laughed because we were all tired—except for Janey. Determined to put a crowning touch of new memories on the day, I asked Mark for his ax (I'd left mine in the car) and after a couple of weak swings—and with the crowd cheering me on—I hacked my way through the trunk of the tree. As the tree separated itself from the base, it was Janey who yelled out "Timber." Sara chose the tree right next to the one Janey had picked and at last our day was complete, our mission a complete success.

We brought our three trees back down the mountain, loaded Gerta's and Janey's into the truck, and then paid Mr. Green; he said we'd picked some nice ones and did as promised, gave us sensible instructions on how to keep them fresh throughout the season.

"And they'll look darned good with lots of tinsel," he told Janey.

"I like tinsel—lots of tinsel," she replied.

We said our good-byes to Mark and Sara, and as we pulled out of the lot, I caught sight of the happy young couple in my rearview mirror. They were locked in a tight embrace, kissing against the mountainous backdrop, snow falling all around them. They resembled something out of a Hollywood movie, the mood perfectly set for romance. That's when I noticed Janey was watching them, too.

"Are they going to get married?" she asked.

"I don't know," I said, wondering what made her think such a thing.

* * *

When we got back to the farmhouse, I asked Janey if she still wanted me to bring her over to Ashley's. She quickly declined. "I don't need to see her, not today." I unloaded the tree from atop the car and removed the strings from its body, placing it in the backyard to allow it to settle back into its proper shape. Then I made some hot chocolate and brought it up to Janey's room, saw that the excitement of the day, or maybe the range of emotions that had toyed with her, had taken its toll. She had fallen asleep. I tossed a blanket over her and closed her bedroom door.

When I returned downstairs, a knock came at the front door. I peered through the curtain, saw that Mark Ravens had dropped by.

"Hey, Mark, come on in," I said, holding open the front door. The temperature had dropped significantly in the hour since coming home.

"Thanks, hope I'm not disturbing you, I know you've got to get to work soon. So do I," he said, removing his winter coat.

Saturday night was one of my nights at the tavern and it was usually one of the busiest. But I had a half hour before I needed to leave, and besides, if I was a few minutes late, it meant Janey could rest that much longer. She was going to have dinner with Gerta and help her with her tree decorating. A new tradition, I had explained to Janey. As it was, Saturday was Gerta's regular night for watching Janey, but this would make it extra special.

"So, Mark, what's up?" I asked, the two of us sitting at the kitchen table. I grabbed two Cokes and set them down.

"It's about Sara."

"I figured. You two have gotten, what should I say, cozier?"

He smiled wide. "Oh, way beyond that, man. Brian, I'm nuts about her. All those times I went to the Five-O over the years, it just never occurred to me to ask her out. I don't why. She was just, you know, one of the girls, a waitress. And then one day she's at the tavern and I can't take my eyes off of her."

"Martha's waitress uniforms are not exactly complimentary."

He laughed. "Well, yeah, that plus the day she brought that food over, guess I started thinking differently about her. But, anyway, what I was wondering about is, you know, that apartment above the bar?"

"I know it very well as a matter of fact," I said. "I lived there when I first moved to Linden Corners, it's a great little place. What, are you interested in renting it?"

"Definitely. I've been saving a lot of cash living with my folks and also what with the holidays here the tips have been good lately—at the bar and down in at the hotel in Hudson. So I'm thinking maybe I can make a go of it, especially if, well, if I ask Sara if she wants to live there with me."

I was struck suddenly by Janey's earlier comment, wondering if these two lovebirds had marriage in their future. If so, I had to give Janey credit for being the astute observer. So I filled Mark in about the apartment's amenities and charms and quirks and suggested one night soon I give him the grand tour, "just so it's the right fit for you. And for Sara."

"Good idea," he said, "though I'm sure it'll be fine. What's the rent?"

"That's up to Gerta. I'm just the hired help; she still owns the building."

"Okay, I'll talk to her about it, thanks, Brian. I can't tell you what a big help you've been to me, and not just today. A few months ago, I had no girlfriend and not much money and suddenly I'm in love and looking for a new place to live. Man, who would thought it, huh? Life can change on a dime, can't it?"

"Sometimes on a nickel," I remarked.

I was happy for him, glad too to have been a part of helping him get on his feet. Linden Corners had embraced me with such ease and genuine warmth it was nice to return the favor, even if Mark wasn't exactly new to town like I'd been.

"Well, duty calls," Mark said, rising from his seat. "Thanks."

"Anytime, Mark. Let me know if Gerta quotes you a stiff price, I'll talk her down a few hundred."

Mark's face temporarily paled, until he realized I'd been kidding.

"I can't spend all my money on rent," he said. "There's Christmas coming, and things can be expensive, if you know what I mean."

As Mark's car pulled out of the driveway, I wandered into the dark living room and took a seat in the recliner. Using what little light was left of the day, I gazed about the room looking for the ideal spot for the tree. But as much as I tried to think about the upcoming holiday, I kept returning to Mark's cryptic comment. *Things* were expensive. Was he planning on buying a ring for Sara?

Life was moving forward for so many. I had to wonder, though, was it for me as well, for Janey? Never in our short-lived relationship had problems existed between us. She was as charmed by me as I was by her, no small feat the former. But it had been like between us from the moment we had met at the base of the windmill. She'd been playing a game that day. Today, though, I'd seen another side of her and it had been no game. I had to hope that I'd seen the last of that behavior.

Like I said, denial has its comforts.

CHAPTER SEVEN

Three nights later, the living room at the farmhouse was in total disarray. Pine needles doubled as a second carpet and boxes that been brought down from the attic were strewn about, half-empty now after nearly two hours of work on mine and Janey's part. The result, though, was a nearly-decorated Christmas tree. The string of lights circled the branches, the golden garland glistened against the array of colored bulbs and shiny ornaments adorned virtually every branch. What remained was the crowning touch—the tinsel. "My favorite," Janey exclaimed, clapping her tiny hands with enthusiasm. Of course I remembered this detail from our trip to Green's Tree Farm and so had bought an extra box, so Janey could go at it to her heart's content.

Which is what she was doing just as the telephone rang. I left her to answer it.

"Hello," I said into the receiver. I had gone to the kitchen to answer.

"Brian, it's your father."

"Oh, hi, Dad," I said. Had I guessed who might have been calling, I would have been wrong no matter the number of chances given. "What a surprise to hear from you."

"Yes, I admit that it's quite rare for me to pick up a phone—unless I need to check on a stock, you know." His question, I assumed, was rhetorical. "Your mother and I are soon to leave for our cruise with the Hendersons, but I was just going over my accounts and I was surprised to learn that you hadn't yet cashed the check I gave you. So I wanted to know if everything was all right."

How stupid of me not to think that he wouldn't notice. "No, no problem, Dad. I just haven't gotten around to it, uh, yet."

"Brian, it's careless to leave a check for such a large amount of money lying around the house. My accountant also doesn't like me having that much money just floating out there in some financial netherworld." He paused. "And the end of the year is coming up."

"Dad, what you gave me is not a tax write off," I said.

But he was moving full steam ahead, no doubt his words scripted in his head. "Brian, presenting you with that check was not meant to hurt your pride. It's, well, like it or not, it's our way of helping you out, of supporting you not just financially but…well, with your decision. Cash the check, have a good Christmas with Janey, and then I'm sure the rest will come in handy in the new year. That's it, Brian, no more lecturing."

"I appreciate your concern, Dad, and I'll head over to the bank tomorrow," I said. "Oh, before you hang up, did you and Mom get the invite? I was hoping, well, you know, maybe you could make it up to Linden Corners before the holiday. The cruise doesn't leave until the twenty-fourth, right? So you could make it; it would be good for you to see where I live, where I work, meet my friends. Maybe have some of my own family around."

"It's a kind invitation, Brian, but at this time of year it's just not doable. Your mother is helping with several charity functions and I've got work piled up—if she and I are going to get away with the Hendersons, we'll need every moment until then. I'm sorry, son."

"That's okay," I said, not surprised by their decision but disappointed nonetheless.

"Good-bye, Brian. And don't forget, first thing tomorrow..."

"I know, go to the bank. Bye, Dad."

I hung up the phone and returned to the living room, where I found Janey sitting on the sofa, strands of tinsel dangling from her fingertips.

"Hey, no breaks. Get to work," I said, jokingly cracking the whip.

"I'm tired," she said. "Can I clean up all this tomorrow?"

"We're almost done," I said, anxiety welling up inside me. Just minutes ago we had been having a grand time, and now she had grown sullen, not even looking my way as she addressed me. I wondered what could possibly have occurred during the time of the phone call and now and came up empty. I tried to coax her into finishing the decorating (and clean up), enticing her with promises of an ice cream sundae—"chocolate syrup and everything—" but she turned me down flat.

"Goodnight, Brian."

I wished her pleasant dreams as she padded her way up the stairs. I heard not another peep out of her the remainder of the night. Frustrated by these sudden shifts in her mood, I busied myself with cleaning up the mess we had made. And when I finished, I turned off the lamp and sat and stared at the sparkling Christmas tree. Thoughts churned in my head, about Janey and about my parents too, trying to figure out what to do with that twenty-five thousand dollar check. I was loathe to accept it, but I'd been left with little choice. My father didn't make phone calls because he enjoyed them.

Maybe it was the phone call from my father that made me remember, but I realized the tree wasn't yet complete, not for me it wasn't. The ornament with my name still sat beneath Janey's bed and I suppose I was waiting for her to finally return it. In fact, I'd hoped having the tree up would inspire her to come around. Still, there was nothing from her camp on the issue. As I sat down on the sofa and looked at the near-finished tree, I had to wonder if my parents, even with their pending trip, were putting up a tree in their new home. Would they dust off their name ornaments, too? Would Rebecca do the same? Did anyone still remember Philip and his gift to the family?

* * *

The next morning, Janey came downstairs already dressed for school. I had breakfast ready, so the two of us sat down at the table. She had a healthy appetite this morning, unlike me. I was still worried about these moods swings, the rift between us. I ate very little. Before she left that morning, she stole a look at the tree.

"Wow, Brian, it's really beautiful, we did a good job."

"It's because of the tinsel—wait until we light it up tonight," I said. "The lights make the shiny ornaments sparkle."

Even as I said it, I cursed my passive aggressive approach. Thing was, Janey bit.

"I feel bad, Brian."

"Why, sweetie?"

"Because you can't find your special ornament," she said, without a hint of remorse. "Oh, well, the bus will be here in moments."

It was almost as if Janey was living in denial as well. She just wouldn't confess that she'd taken it.

After she left, I considered going up to her room and retrieving the box from underneath her bed and just placing the ornament on the tree. Then I could gauge Janey's reaction. But how would I explain the presence of the ornament, that I had been searching her room? That I was cleaning and found it? Even in my mind that excuse sounded hollow. No easy solution presented itself to me, so I busied myself with other matters.

I had the day to myself. Around ten that morning I trekked through the snowy field, heading for the windmill. Now that the farmhouse was all decorated for the season, there was nothing left to do in preparation for Christmas. Even the shopping was mostly done. As I made my way down the hill, the sight of the windmill made me take a step back, like always. The sails were quiet, barely moving on this especially calm day. A rich, blue hue coated the sky and the air contained a crispness that chilled my bones; I could easily see my breath in front of me. But what struck me most was that, in this season of gleaming lights and abundant joy, the windmill looked lonely and forgotten, somehow colorless. It hadn't occurred to me to ask whether Annie decorated the windmill during the holiday season. If she did, was it for her pleasure or for the enjoyment of passing motorists who could see the great mill from the road. Blinking lights of blue and green and red and yellow struck me as the wrong chord. But maybe something more sedate. And, as though the windmill had inspired me, I found myself liking more and more the picture my mind had conjured.

To turn my new dream to reality, there was an errand I needed to run. I had to go to town anyway—a trip to the bank nagged. I could stop by Ackroyd's Hardware Emporium as well to get the necessary materials for giving the windmill a holiday sparkle. Energized now, I returned to the farmhouse, grabbed the check my father had given me and hopped into the car. I found myself humming Christmas songs the entire trip into town, the holiday spirit awakened within me. As I parked the car and headed up the sidewalk to the Columbia County Savings Bank, I nearly ran into Cynthia Knight.

"Hey, Brian, look out."

"Oh, hey, Cyn, sorry. Guess I'm a little distracted."

"A little?"

I smiled. "Some last minute details to attend to."

"Well, I'm glad I ran into you. I've got some last minute shopping to do at the mall and I was planning to go tomorrow afternoon. Bradley needs some new shirts and he hates department stores, so I thought I'd wrap up a few for under the tree. Men are so difficult to buy for. Would you like that, if someone bought you new dress shirts for Christmas?"

"I don't wear dress shirts anymore, so no, I wouldn't like them."

"Real helpful," she said, punching me lightly. "Anyway, I was thinking maybe Janey would want to join me—do you think she'll hate that?"

I laughed. "Hate going to the mall? Janey'll love it."

"Good. I figured maybe she needed to do some shopping of her own," Cynthia said, sporting a knowing look. My guess was, this plan had already been discussed and needed only my approval. "Also, there's that gift drive sponsored by St. Matthew's, it's good for every kid to contribute to the less fortunate ones. I need a kid's opinion on what another kid would like."

"Good idea," I said. "Thanks, Cyn, Janey will have a ball."

She returned to her car and I realized I had lost an opportunity to ask Cynthia if she had detected a change in Janey's behavior; or was it reserved only for me? I could have solicited her opinion on what might be bothering Janey, but in the end I was glad I hadn't. Cynthia had taken on enough responsibility in helping out with Janey, the last thing she needed to hear about was my insecurity. Janey and I would make it through, we were a team. The conviction I felt was not as strong as I might have wished it.

Pushing those thoughts to the back of my mind, I went inside the bank, filled out a deposit slip and then handed it and the check to the teller. The teller raised her eyes at the amount, but said nothing, he just took care of the paperwork.

"Will there be anything else, Mr. Duncan?"

"As a matter of fact," I said, sudden inspiration hitting me, "there is."

A few minutes later I left, the distaste in my mouth starting to clear. I headed for the hardware store, leaving my car in the bank's lot for the quick walk across the street. Linden Corners's downtown area was that easily negotiated.

Ackroyd's Hardware Emporium was owned by Chuck Ackroyd, a long-time resident of Linden Corners and not my biggest fan, even though we had seen each other through the fiercest of storms last summer, a rare meeting of our minds. He had been one of George's regulars, one of his friends, too, and resentment had reared its ugly head once George embraced me as he did. As I walked into Chuck's store that day, the bells jangling above my head, I saw him standing at the information desk. I nodded hello, and he busied himself with something other than saying hello back. Not even the holiday season could help him, though in fairness to him, he had no one in which to share it. His wife had run out on him years ago and he hadn't fully swallowed that bitter pill.

I went down the aisle filled with Christmas accoutrements and picked out several boxes of white lights, then went in search of extension cords and more staples for the gun. When I had all I required, I made my way to the cashier and paid for them. Chuck came by to bag my purchases, casting me a wide eye as he stuffed the numerous lights into the brown paper bag.

"You lighting up the sky with these?" he asked.

"No, just the windmill."

He harrumphed. "You and that windmill. I don't get it."

"Merry Christmas to you too, Chuck" I replied, wishing I hadn't allowed him to goad me. I turned all smiles then and said, "So, see you at the party this weekend?"

He shrugged. "Probably not."

I was about to brush him off, but that's what he expected me to do. Instead, I said, "We would like you to be there. Your invitation might have been sent by me, but it really comes from Gerta. She considers you a dear friend of the family; you were there for her during the funeral and after. This year's party is another passage for her, her first without George. Don't disappoint her, Chuck. Besides, you never know who'll show up, maybe make you smile."

"I'll think about it," he said.

Well, there's progress for you.

When I returned home, I hid the lights inside the windmill alongside Janey's presents. She came home from school a couple hours later, Ashley in tow. Oh goody, my favorite person. She hadn't asked in advance if her friend could come over, but I chose to say nothing. Janey was happily showing off the Christmas tree, informing her friend that she had hung most of the ornaments herself. Nothing was said about the one ornament that was missing. "Brian was busy, talking with his father on the phone," she said, making sure I overheard her. The exaggerated comment penetrated my skin, my heart taking a direct hit. When Ashley's mother came to pick her up, Ashley stuck her tongue out at me. It was getting to be a habit with her.

Later, when Janey was getting ready for bed, I sat on the edge of the bed as I usually did.

"You had a good day?" I asked her.

"Uh-huh. I like when Ashley comes over to play, she's fun to be with," she said. "And I'm sorry I forgot to tell you she was coming. That wasn't very nice of me."

"Just remember that for the next time."

"I will," she said, and her voice was so filled with sadness I felt a need to cheer her up.

So I told her then about Cynthia's idea of a trip to the mall tomorrow afternoon, which excited Janey; she had something to look forward to.

"And who knows, maybe they'll be a surprise waiting for you when you return."

Her eyes lit up. "Can you give me a hint?"

"As a matter of fact, no I cannot. Consider it something special to dream about," I said, then kissed her on the top of her head. As I was leaving her room, I turned back, saw the whites of her eyes staring up at me through the darkness.

"What is it?" I asked, wondering if this was the moment of truth. She'd apologized for her thoughtless behavior, for bringing Ashley over without asking. So I had to hope that would open the floodgates for more truths.

She hesitated and in the end just shook her head. "Nothing."

"You sure?" I asked.

"Yes, Brian. But thanks, I know you're always there for me."

Despite the conflicts that ran through me, I let it go. "Okay. Good-night, Janey Sullivan. I love you."

"Good-night, Brian Duncan. I love you more."

Seemed to be a day for progress.

* * *

Janey had her instructions to go directly to Cynthia's after school, do not pass "Go," do not collect two hundred dollars, and most certainly, do NOT come to the farmhouse, "because I won't be there then." That was a necessary white lie, because the notion of putting up lights all around the windmill was daunting at best and I needed all the time I could get to do it right. Decorating the tavern had taken an entire morning and that wasn't nearly the number of lights I was planning to use for this project. I had a lot of stapling ahead of me. Fortunately, the weather chose to cooperate and the arctic air that had settled over the region these past few days dissipated, giving me workable temperatures in the high thirties. Still not ideal, but better than twenty with a worse wind chill.

I had all the tools necessary down at the windmill. Two ladders, the staple gun, the lights and extension cords I had bought, as well as a thermos of hot coffee to keep me warm from the inside. So at nine o'clock I began to work and as the clock ticked, so did the staple gun, as I placed strings of lights all over—on the tower, the cap, the windows of the mill. What I couldn't figure out was how to get them on the sails; that was just too impossible a task, since their constant rotation would just get the wires all tangled. It was a logistical problem that continued to elude me as the day progressed, and as lunchtime approached, I was still without a solution. I took a break by returning to the farmhouse.

I wasn't in the kitchen two minutes before I saw Gerta's car pull up the driveway. She stepped out, carrying in her hands one of her famously delicious strawberry pies.

"Well, this is a surprise," I said, opening the front door. I tried to take the pie from her hands, but she said she could manage.

"I made several for the party, but I knew to save one for you, dear," she explained, setting it on the kitchen counter before offering up a kiss to my cheek. "My goodness, Brian, you're frozen solid. What have you been doing, sleeping on ice?"

"Hardly, but I have been outside most of the day. You know, you're not the only one with surprises," I said. "But if you want to come back later today, around sundown, you can see for yourself what I've been doing."

"Very intriguing, Brian. But very well. I've got some shopping to do."

"Got time for lunch first?"

"Are you cooking?" she asked warily.

"Hey, I'm getting better at that stuff. Besides, I was only going to make a sandwich. How badly could I mess that up?"

So Gerta joined me for a quick meal, and as we ate she continued to prod me into confessing what I'd been working. I continued to smile but say nothing and eventually she changed the subject.

"Oh, Brian, I meant to talk to you. Mark Ravens came to see me, asking about the apartment above the bar. I told him to talk to you about all the details, but he said you had referred him to me. Goodness, what do I know about things such as rent. Are utilities included, or are they extra? How would I know those answers?

George handled that kind of stuff. And since you were the previous tenant, I would think you'd have a better sense of those details, certainly more than me. I told Mark I'd get back to him. But really, Brian, I've given you free reign over the tavern. The decisions are yours."

"I know you've said so, but Gerta, that bar is part of your family's legacy. I'm the caretaker. You're the caregiver."

"Hmm, seems I'm going to have a make a decision after all."

As we finished our sandwiches, I suggested dessert.

"I know you, Brian Duncan, you're just looking for an excuse to cut into that pie. Don't let me stop you." She paused. "But you better cut two pieces."

Gerta left shortly afterwards, and I returned to the windmill, where I spent the next three hours putting up the last of the lights, finishing with the railing that encircled the outer catwalk. At last, I was out of lights and had made all the necessary electrical connections. I ran the extension cords inside and plugged them into the available sockets. Fortunately the windmill had working electricity and I only hoped whatever circuit breaker they were on could handle the amount of power required.

When I had put away all the tools, I returned to the windmill and went up to Annie' studio.

"Well, Annie, I don't know what kind of traditions you and Janey had when it came to the windmill, but, well, here's a new one, I hope. New traditions are good, they give you a sense that, even though it's the first time, there is intent for something longer, something everlasting. I only wish I could have lit up the sails, how beautiful they would have looked against the dark sky."

Darkness finally settled upon the snowy valley. Back inside the warmth of the farmhouse, I waited for Janey's return, and at six-thirty I heard tires crunching against the gravel driveway. I went out to meet Cynthia and Janey, and like clockwork, behind them in pulled Gerta. She had run into them at the mall, conveniently enough.

"Janey wanted to watch the little kids visit Santa," Cynthia said.

"And then Gerta walked right past us," Janey said.

"Okay, Windmill Man," Gerta said. "What's the surprise."

"Ooh, yeah, the surprise! I want to see it, too!" Janey exclaimed.

Cynthia tossed me a look. "It's all she's been talking about all day."

"Then let's not waste another minute. Follow me," I said.

And they did, the four of us trudging through the snowy field, down the hill, the moon our only guide on this blackest of nights. Winter had officially arrived today and snow was in the forecast, the cloud cover keeping the stars at bay.

"Okay, stay there," I said to the three ladies in my life, feeling like a kid at Christmas who couldn't wait for someone to open a gift I'd gotten them. Because I knew how special it was and I wanted to share it with them.

I dashed inside the windmill. The surge protector was turned off, but the extension cords were already plugged in. All it took was one flick of the switch, and I readied my finger, praying that this went off in real life as successfully as it had in my mind. Then I depressed the red button and even though I was inside the darkened windmill, suddenly I was cast in warm light. From outside I heard a loud exclamation. Like a crowd reacting to fireworks. I ran back out and joined them, staring at the windmill, itself lit like a giant spinning angel against the heavens.

"Oh, Brian..."

"Wow..."

"Sweet Lord..."

So said Cynthia, Janey, Gerta, respectively, and as they reacted I studied the results of my handiwork. The windmill was ablaze with white light from top to bottom, hundreds of twinkling stars, as though they had fallen from the sky to brighten this cold night. And even though the sails themselves held no lights, what I'd inadvertently created was a magical shadow effect, with the bright glare of the lights that adorned the tower emitting strong beams that, set against the dark blanket of night, were thrust through the sails. And as the wind picked up and the sails turned, the light flickered against the ground, shadows dancing amidst us. The effect was more than I could have wished for, and as the light reflected against our awed faces, I couldn't help but think of Annie, of her special spirit, how it inspired me and how it fed me such strength. As if reading my thoughts, Janey came to my side and wrapped her arms around me. I held her tight, and for a moment the world consisted of only the two of us, Janey and Brian, and in our eyes and our hearts was Annie, the woman who had brought us together. Annie had blessed us today, on what was supposedly the shortest day of the year, one I wished could have lasted forever.

CHAPTER EIGHT

The magical night we lit the windmill wasn't over, not yet. The four of us stood for who knew how long, marveling at the illumination before us, basking in its magnetic glow before finally feeling the evening's cold penetrate through the layers of clothing we wore. The wind had definitely picked up and snow flakes had begun to drift down from the sky. I invited them all back to the farmhouse, where we made good use of the strawberry pie Gerta had brought over earlier. Gerta, though, was growing tired and so she left shortly afterwards, saying she'd see us tomorrow at the tavern.

After she'd gone, Cynthia said to me, "Brian, she's so looking forward to the party—I think she had given up hope of having her annual celebration. Connors' Corner might have been George's domain the rest of the year, but on that particular night it was Gerta who ran the place with a smile as addictive as her pies. And she loved every minute of it."

"Well, I'll be busy behind the bar and so will Mark, who arranged to get the night off from his hotel job just so he could help out. Though I suspect he has ulterior motives." I paused, taking a sip from my mug of tea. "So, that will allow Gerta to play lady of the manor and welcome all our guests. It should be fun."

"What will?" Janey said, bringing in her empty pie plate from the living room.

"The big party tomorrow," I said. "You ready for it?"

"You bet."

"Good," I said, "so what do you say, you get a good night's rest in preparation. It's already been a big day, and tomorrow promises to be bigger."

She rolled her eyes and said to Cynthia, "He's not very subtle."

"Ha-ha, off to bed Little Miss Big Words," I said, pretending to chase after her. She went running up the stairs, squealing with delight. I told her I'd be up in a minute, then asked if Cynthia minded staying for awhile longer.

"I was planning to, if you don't mind—I want to talk to you about something."

Curious about what might be on her mind, I told her to hold that thought while I went to check on Janey. By the time I got upstairs Janey had already brushed her teeth and thrown her pajamas on and was settled under the covers with her book. We talked for just a couple minutes, because even though her pleas of wanting to stay awake said otherwise, her yawns betrayed her. As I got up from the bed, she said, "Thanks, Brian, for making the windmill sparkle so beautifully. Momma would have loved it."

"It sure is bright, no doubt she can see it its glow from way above; I'm sure she's smiling right now."

I flicked off the light, closed the door, and with a full heart returned to the kitchen. Cynthia was pouring herself a fresh mug of tea.

"I'll take a refill," I said.

We sat down at the table, both of us ready to dig into the topic we each wished to discuss. Which turned out to be the same.

"I want to talk about Janey," we both said, and then laughed.

"You first, Brian, what's going on?"

Despite my earlier reservations about involving Cynthia, I knew I needed some womanly wisdom. So I told her about the shifts in mood and the attitude, the brashness with which Janey wore her limited independence. "It's been unpredictable, Cyn. Some nights—like tonight—we're totally fine, and then others, yikes, she won't even listen to me. Maybe it's the stress of the holidays, or maybe she misses Annie so much she's uncertain how to deal with her emotions. Whatever's truly bothering her, it's not good for her—not good for us. Janey and I are only going to work if we can keep open the lines of communication. And that's what she doesn't do, communicate. She shuts down."

"Have you said anything to her?" she asked.

I confessed to Cynthia that I tended to avoid confrontation, that was my style. "Always has been," I said, thinking of how quietly I'd left New York. There had been no big blow ups, no arguments, I had become an emotional steel trap and no animal dared penetrate. That's when I realized I was doing the same. And both Janey and Cynthia seemed to have recognized that. I told her then about the case of the missing Christmas ornament, of my fears and my avoidance. "I don't want to upset the delicate balance that already exists between us. And I know how silly this sounds, it's just a stupid tree ornament."

"No, Brian, it's anything but silly—or stupid. Obviously the ornament is important to you, otherwise you might have dealt with the issue already. Maybe you're not ready to speak of its significance, that's why you're letting it remain unnoticed under her bed. But you do need to clear this matter up—and fast. You can't have those suspicions hanging over you, it will damage this Christmas and maybe all the others, too. Get the ornament back first of all; then you need to talk to Janey about it. But I'll tell you, Brian, she's mentioned the ornament to me and all she's ever said was how pretty it is. I didn't sense that there was something wrong there," Cynthia said, pausing. "As for the behavioral fluctuations, well, let me approach this from another angle and see if we can't find some common road. Today at the mall, it was all I could do to keep her focused on the gift-buying. All she wanted to do was look at the people—mostly at couples. Holding hands or even kissing and she would make comments, like..."

"Like they were going to get married."

"She's done that with you, too?"

I related the story of seeing Mark and Sara at the tree farm, ending with Janey's question about their possible marriage. "It seemed to come out of left field, Cyn. But then Mark comes to me later that same day, asking to rent the apartment above the tavern. He's going to ask Sara to move in with him, and I wondered if maybe there was more to his actions. He practically admitted to getting ready to propose. How Janey guessed it, I don't know."

"Obviously, it's what's picking at her mind, whether she realizes it or not. Her actions toward you—that brashness you spoke of—might not be so deliberate, Brian. Perhaps her subconscious is playing tricks with her, making her act out. Even she might not understand why she's saying what she is."

I shrugged. "I'm hardly a trained psychologist—add in the complex workings of a child's mind and well, we'd have an easier time with a thousand piece jigsaw puzzle of a blizzard."

She laughed. "Well, I wish I had a perfect solution for you."

"No, Cynthia, it helps just being able to talk about it. It's just something I'm going to have to watch out for over time, and if it persists—or worsens, God forbid—then I'll have to take some kind of action. Who knows, maybe if we talk about the ornament, everything else will fall into place. I'm sure it's all wrapped up under one big 'issue' somewhere in her mind. For now, I just want to get through Christmas."

"You know, that could be it, too, Brian. She did confess one thing to me."

"What's that?"

"She said, and I quote, 'For Christmas, I want to give Brian what he most wants.'"

"And did she offer up what that was?"

"Nope."

"Hmm, the plot thickens," I said.

Cynthia left a few minutes later, leaving me with a sink full of dirty dishes and a mind full of unanswered, nagging questions. I went upstairs, checked on Janey, who was fast asleep. Her purple frog, though, had fallen to the floor and I bent down to retrieve it. After placing the frog back in her arms, I returned my attention back to underneath her bed. Tucked against the bedpost was the little brown cardboard box, still undisturbed from when I'd discovered it earlier. Hearing Cynthia's words in my head, I realized that she was right, I needed to just take back the ornament. There was no more delaying the issue; no more denials.

And so I withdrew the box from its hiding place, my hands shaking as I opened the lid. My mouth dropped as I stared inside the box—the empty box. The Christmas ornament wasn't inside it. My heart sunk as I considered what next I should do. Afraid now that Janey might awaken, I returned the box to where I'd found it and quickly left the room. When finally I slipped beneath the covers of my own bed, I wondered if I could possibly have dreamed up the discovery and knew that was just wishful thinking. Here was a further complication I hadn't expected.

The box had been there all along. But where was the ornament?

* * *

So the day of the annual George's Tavern Christmas party finally arrived, and there was so much preparation involved, Janey and I barely saw each other that day. She and I needed to talk, that much was obvious, but the timing had to be just right—no distractions. There was no denying I was devastated by this latest turn of events regarding the ornament, and as Mark and I went about our routine of checking the taps, dusting the bottles and shining up the bar, I found myself walking around in a fog.

"Hey, Bri—you with us today?"

"Yeah," I answered automatically. "Why?"

"Well, you're polishing the plastic pitchers."

So I was. I put down both towel and pitcher and suggested a break. "I could use one," I said.

"How 'bout you show me the apartment now?" Mark said.

"Great idea."

It was three in the afternoon, an hour away from the start of the party. Cynthia Knight had volunteered to help Gerta bring over the food and her husband, Bradley, had gone to St. Matthew's to borrow a long table in which to set out the delicious buffet. So, with the bar all ready for a long night of revelers, I grabbed the keys out of the register and waved Mark onward.

"I haven't been upstairs in a while, so it might be a bit musty."

Mark didn't care, he was twenty-four and on the verge of getting his first apartment. The roaches could have given him a welcome parade and we'd have been thrilled; not that we had roaches here at the tavern. There were two ways to get to the upstairs, through a door that was right off the rear bar, or through a separate back entrance. It consisted of three rooms—a bedroom, living room, and eat-in-kitchen, each room generous with its allotted space. Furniture came with the place, I said as we headed up the stairs, "but of course, if you want to replace it with some of your own, go ahead. I'll just store the stuff in my barn."

"Oh no, I don't have anything."

"Well, Sara might," I said.

He nodded eagerly, "Oh yeah, right. Not that I've said anything, not yet."

"Your secret is safe with me."

With a flourish, I threw open the door to the apartment and allowed Mark to step in first. He gazed around, his grin increasing the further he ventured forward. He gave the place a good inspection, and as he did, I allowed the memories of this past summer to wash over me. What a terrific place this apartment had been, just enough space so I hadn't felt cramped, but not too big that I got lost. My needs had been simple then, a perfect match for a home that needed only a willing tenant. And judging from Mark's reaction, the apartment had found its newest occupant. I was glad to help him move forward with his life.

"How long did you live here?" he asked me.

"I don't know, let me see. Five months, until I moved into the farmhouse."

"Right. And what about all those nights you didn't work at the bar, was the noise loud?"

"You can't hear a thing. Good solid floors, along with the two doors at either end of the staircase, manage to keep out all sound from below. And I would assume vice versa."

Mark grinned. "I'll take it."

"We haven't talked about the monthly rate. Gerta asked me to handle it."

"So she said. But no worries, I'll take it," he repeated.

And so he did. We agreed to work out the particulars later and I agreed to be fair with the rent. Then we returned to the bar, where Gerta and Cynthia were already busy bringing in dishes, and Bradley had set up the metal folding table against the far wall. I had at least proved my point, that you couldn't hear a darn thing that went on below.

In any case, Christmas was just two days away and Linden Corners was ready to celebrate this most special holiday, where families joined together for a joyous time and friends became that much closer. George's Tavern, while a place for adults on every other occasion, this day we were open to the entire public; we were about community, not alcohol, though that wasn't to say we weren't serving. The food was on us, the drinks on whomever wanted one, that was the deal and we received nary a complaint. By six that evening the tavern was filled, the jukebox was playing only Christmas-themed songs, people were engaged in games of pool or were talking at tables, against the wall, at the bar. The mood was festive and it had an infectious hold over me. I pulled the tap with a smile, filling and refilling glasses, just like George had taught me last summer. And Gerta, she stood over the trays of food—a glazed ham, fried chicken and plates of lasagna, sausages and peppers and potatoes and vegetables, breads and rolls and for dessert, pies and lots of 'em. A veritable feast for a variety of folks.

My regulars had all turned out, even Chuck Ackroyd showed up, who was busy talking with Martha Martinson.

"Good thing Gerta only does this once a year, she's better at cooking than I am at telling jokes," Martha said, her fingers licking away the grease from a piece of chicken.

A dreamy-eyed Sara Joyner was there, hanging out at the edge of the bar, talking with Mark whenever he got a free moment. Marla and Darla, who owned the shops down the street, could always be counted on for a party, and just as they had done last summer at First Friday, they sat there doing tequila shots and trying to outdo the other. Bradley and Cynthia Knight were dancing to the Eurythmics version of "Winter Wonderland," which had slowed the party's tone down some.

"Hey, we worked hard," Bradley said, "So I've earned a slow dance with my lovely wife."

The song ended and then the joint was rocking again, with Bruce Springsteen's "Santa Claus is Coming to Town."

At six-thirty, I was about to offer Mark a break when a surprise guest arrived through the front door and my mouth nearly dropped. It was my friend John Oliver, and at his side was a smiling Anna. I informed Mark that I was taking the break instead, and went over to greet my friend with a huge welcoming hug.

"Man, I can't believe you're here—is this some dream?"

"Where are the cows, Bri?"

Anna slapped him, saying, "You said no farm jokes."

But that was okay, we all laughed and then I escorted them to the bar, where I asked the twins to give up their seats for a while. I gave them a complimentary shot and they acquiesced, jointly stumbling off to get some food. John was impressed with my managerial skills, less so with my bartending skills.

"Where are our freebies? We drove all this way."

So I poured John a draft and got Anna her requested glass of Chardonnay, warning her that, "Wine's not our specialty," and then set about taking care of introductions. John met Gerta and Cynthia and Bradley, even Chuck came over to say hello, more interested in Anna's form than in meeting the guy with the arm wrapped around her. "They sure got pretty women in that city," was his comment; he'd been equally taken with Maddie when she'd made a surprise, last-ditch visit last summer. With John here, though, it was the perfect mingling of my old world and my new life.

"Where's Janey?" John asked.

"With her friend, Ashley," I said. "Her parents promised to come by for dinner around seven, let the kids dance and have fun for a couple hours. Probably good that she's not here the entire time, I've been swamped since we opened the doors. Hey, I'm glad you're here, John, it means the world to me."

"No problem," he said. "But I hope there are some accommodations in this rinky-dink town of yours. Some place called the Solemn Nights was all booked."

"Stay at the farmhouse, no debate. You're better off."

With those details settled on, John and Anna got some food and started to mingle with the townsfolk of Linden Corners, my friends easily welcoming the newcomers, especially after I announced, "These are my friends from the city and they want to go cow tipping later." That got a huge laugh and before long the city slickers were engulfed in a group of locals who began to debate the plusses and minuses of country life.

Janey showed up finally, with Ashley and her parents, Chris and Lea Baker, nice church-going folk who I don't think had ever stepped foot inside this bar or any other. They had met at church, she taught Sunday school and he helped out with confirmation classes, or so they told me one day when I'd picked up Janey from their house. As they helped themselves to food and sipped at soft drinks, Ashley turned around and stuck out her tongue again. This time I fought back. I stuck my tongue out at her.

Janey, though, didn't notice either exchange. She was all smiles, especially when I brought her behind the bar. I let her pour sodas for herself and Ashley.

"Wow, Brian, I think the entire town is here tonight. Wait, is that John? Oh my God, Anna!" she screamed out from the bar, waving as she did so.

And so Janey was sucked into their world, and I could tell she was clearly delighted to see Anna again. Relief flooded over me as I realized the Janey we all knew and loved had showed up. She was a natural at working the crowd, charming them with her little giggle. As I watched from my post, I at last offered Mark the break I'd promised him. He tossed his dirtied apron on the shelf under the bar, pulling out from a hidden spot behind some bottles a small vial of cologne. He splashed it on, then shrugged when he saw me watching.

"Hey, it was good enough for Sam Malone on 'Cheers,'" he remarked.

He disappeared into the jovial crowd, Sara close behind him, her shriek momentarily rising above the noise from the jukebox.

As more people arrived, Gerta stepped in to help behind the bar and with her at my side, time passed quickly, easily, and before long another hour had passed and Mark hadn't yet returned. Not that I minded, in truth he wasn't even scheduled to work tonight, he was doing this as a favor mostly (though he was working for tips, which tonight were beyond good). I was about to send out a search party for him when another surprise presented itself to me. My mouth hung so wide open, I might have been catching barflies.

"Rebecca?" I mouthed, and then realized that's exactly who had just walked through the front entrance of George's Tavern. My sister, and behind her was her son, Junior, a small, wiry kid with dark hair and glasses. Thrust into such unfamiliar surroundings, the din of the crowd and the music blaring, it was no wonder he clung close to his mother.

"Hey, if it isn't Uncle Brian—look at him, Junior, right there behind the bar."

I hadn't seen Junior in over a year, and so his welcome was anything but enthusiastic. But he did shake my hand with a surprisingly firm grip, and in return I tousled his hair, hoping to get a smile. He tried a tiny one before giving up. My sister I hugged, which was rare as well. But I was overcome by the fact that they had showed up. My parents being here I had considered a long shot, Rebecca's presence a near impossibility. Sometimes, though, people surprise you and in a good way.

"We would have been here sooner but I got lost," she said. "Thankfully my headlights caught sight of that windmill you're always talking about—otherwise I might not have known we had found what we were looking for. A blinked, thought I had missed it. It's a really small town, Brian." Then she gazed about the room. "Not that you can tell with the number of people here. Let me guess, free booze?"

"Ha. Free food, yes. The booze you gotta pay for."

"Even for family?"

I mixed a cranberry and vodka for Rebecca, then a Coke for Junior, and when they were settled with some food I called Janey over. Surprise was written across her face when she saw Rebecca, but at least she remembered her and politely said hello. I introduced Janey to Junior, glad to finally do so after Rebecca had failed to bring him to Thanksgiving. Junior was ten years old and just a couple inches taller than Janey. He was more shy, too.

"I'm playing with my friend, Ashley, but you can join us. Wanna pick out some songs on the jukebox?"

"Can I, Mother?"

Rebecca gave him a dollar, "Have fun, Junior. Take good care of him, won't you, Janey?"

The kids went running off, and after I served a couple of patrons I returned to my sister's side to sneak in a moment's conversation. Our parents had left for their cruise, her ex-husband was off to see his own parents somewhere out west, leaving Rebecca and Junior alone for the holidays. "So I figured, why not, Janey and

Junior would meet eventually, so why not take care of it now? And I wanted to see what this windmill thing was all about. Though I'd like to see it up close in the daylight."

"You couldn't see it with all those lights?"

She had no idea what I was talking about, and then I realized that in my haste today to get everything ready for the party, I had forgotten to flip the power switch. On a day filled with celebration, of family, the windmill tonight stood quiet against a dark sky, alone. A waft of sadness washed over me but there was nothing I could do about it now. I assured Rebecca she would see the windmill before night's end, "and don't worry, it's quite a sight."

While we talked and while she drank, I learned that she had dumped that guy Rex soon after Thanksgiving. "We were never serious, I just brought him to piss mother off. She hates the men I date; the ones I marry, too—which is not always mutually exclusive. It's nice to give her something to complain about. For us it's conversation. Ol' Rex served his purpose—in many ways and many times." Ignoring her crass innuendo, I insisted that she and Junior stay overnight at the farmhouse, thrilled by the idea of having a houseful of guests.

As I'd been talking with Rebecca, a flushed Mark Ravens returned to his post behind the bar, and a short while later Sara resurfaced. Her hair was slightly askew and I didn't have to venture a second guess about where they'd been and what they'd been doing. Good solid walls, indeed. So I took that moment to take a break myself, wandering outside to get some fresh air. I left Rebecca talking with, of all people, Chuck Ackroyd, who wanted to know "Is this pretty lady from the city too." I decided to let him discover on his own that she was family.

Snow was falling, cars and sidewalks lightly coated. Though I didn't have a coat on, after the heat of the bar I welcomed the bracing air. I stepped off the porch and wandered away from the building, glad to have a moment to myself. There was no denying that the annual tavern party was a smashing success, and apparently I'd done a good enough job of telling my friends and family how important it was to me. That John and Anna were here was remarkable; Rebecca bringing Junior so he could meet Janey, that was one for the ages.

I was feeling the chill now and remembered I'd left my coat in my car. I went to retrieve it. Small voices coming from the back steps halted my progress. I recognized Janey's. I was about to make a hasty retreat when I heard the word, "father," which made me stop in my tracks. If I made a noise, I might be discovered and that would be far worse than what I was really doing.

Because I was curious to hear what she had to say, and while eavesdropping wasn't in my nature, given all that had been going on between me and Janey perhaps I might gain a little insight. So I listened in.

"He's not, you know, my father," Janey said.

"I didn't think so," said Junior, his squeaky voice distinctive. "I mean, I haven't seen Uncle Brian in, uh, well, at least a year and I didn't remember him having a kid. Or being married. He was always the guy we saw at Christmas, or sometimes visited in his tiny New York apartment. So you can't just show up one day with a... eight year old girl and say 'Look, I have a kid.'"

"Nope."

"So what happened?"

"My real father died several years ago, I don't remember him so much, I was so young. But my momma, a bad thing happened to her—not long ago. It's probably not nice to say, but I miss her more. My father I know through the stories Momma told me and the pictures she showed me and just a few of my own memories of him. But Momma? I have lots of memories of her. What about you, you're lucky—you have both a mom and a dad."

"Except they don't live together. It's because they always fight, and sometimes those fights are even about me," said Junior. "I think you're the lucky one, I like Uncle Brian. He's..."

"Silly," Janey said.

"Yeah."

"But he's very good to me, Junior. He makes me pancakes for breakfast whenever I want and he takes me on trips—I went to New York City and saw the biggest Christmas tree ever—and one day all we did all day was go sledding."

"Sounds like a Dad to me," he said.

"Except he's not." There was a moment's pause and then I heard Janey say, "Do you think it's possible someone can have a father and a Dad?"

"Maybe. I mean, my father will always be my father, but sometimes when my mother gets a new boyfriend she asks me whether I wouldn't mind having a 'Dad' around the house. That's what she calls them. Luckily she's in between 'Dad's' right now, so it will be just her and me for Christmas."

"Did you decorate a tree?"

"Yeah, even though we're not home to see it. She insisted, 'cause we had to hang our special decorations."

"An ornament with your name of it?" Janey asked.

My ears perked up, hoping for some new information.

Junior said, "I got mine the year I was born—I'm supposed to think about my Uncle Philip when I hang the ornament but I didn't even know him. So I just try and find a high branch and hope that I'm taller than the year before."

I had heard enough, and certainly I didn't want to be discovered. I crouched back to the front of the building as quietly as possible, and before I returned to the bar I knew I had to wipe my eyes. Tears had started to flow as I'd listened to them, these two complete strangers, bonding now over the saddest idea imaginable, the notion of lost parents. I was grateful to Junior, who had miraculously gotten Janey talking, thinking maybe now that he'd opened the dam, the flood might pass through and find its way to me. So Janey and I could heal whatever riff had come between us.

The rest of the night passed in a blur, so focused on Janey was I. The food was gone and the number of guests had begun to dwindle. Ashley and her parents were long gone, but Janey had opted to stay and she and Junior were playing cards quietly at a table in the corner. When, at eleven, I realized they were still wide awake I suggested maybe it was time to get them back to the farmhouse. They'd probably crash the moment we got back. I mentioned this to Mark, who said no problem, he'd close up.

"But I have one big announcement to make," he said, and then, because he wanted the remaining crowd to hear, he climbed on top of the bar and whistled for everyone to quiet down. Someone pulled the plug on the jukebox and suddenly the bar was awash with rapt silence, everyone staring up expectantly at Mark. I caught a glimpse of Sara out of the corner of my eye, saw the smile that lit her face and guessed what was coming. And indeed I was right, as Mark announced that not only were he and Sara moving into the apartment upstairs the first of the year, they were engaged to be married.

"I couldn't wait until Christmas morning," he said.

"And I couldn't wait to say yes," Sara said, joining her new fiancé atop the bar, where they hugged and kissed amidst a chorus of cheers.

As the crowd quieted down and encircled the happy couple, Cynthia came up to me and said she was going to take Janey back to her place.

"Stay, enjoy yourself, Brian. Janey can stay with me and Bradley tonight, she can even invite Junior over. We've had a nice chat, the three of us. Bradley doesn't mind—when does he, the saint—and that will give you more time with your friends and your sister. Rebecca's quite a character, Bri—I think she's been flirting with Chuck all night. He's completely in the dark about who she is, too, isn't that a riot?"

We shared a good laugh over that. Then, before I gave my blessing to this sudden sleepover, I pulled Janey aside and asked her if she was okay with this.

"Yeah, don't worry, Brian, you have other people to take care of tonight."

Her words stung me, as though I had anyone more important to worry over, to take care of. She was my life and she was drifting away from me. And with tomorrow being Christmas Eve, I felt fear grip my heart—the hoped for joyous holiday wasn't happening. Just the reverse and there seemed nothing I could to stop it.

"See you tomorrow," I said, and watched as Janey went out the door with Cynthia and Bradley, Junior happily trailing right behind them. Rebecca hadn't a problem with the arrangement, and I suspected she was just gearing up for a night of partying. Me, the party mood had just seeped out of me, and I tossed down my apron in frustration.

Mark had the bar and Gerta offered to help him out, "Go ahead, Brian, you look exhausted."

I left the tavern ten minutes later, bringing with me Rebecca and John and Anna, my past suddenly alive in Linden Corners. We did not go directly to the farmhouse, and instead I drove them to the edge of the open field where we could see the giant windmill in the near distance. Even though the snow continued to fall, I asked them all to sit on the hood of their cars and "just wait." I went running across the field, unlocked the front door of the windmill and finally flicked on the light switch. Suddenly the world was lit with hundreds of bright white lights, and I dashed back to rejoin my friends and sister, all of whom were awed by the brilliant sight before us, the sails spinning, the falling snow like chilled fireflies.

"This is where I come to think—to the windmill, because it's where Annie is, and she helps me. It was Annie who dubbed this place 'Brian's Bluff.' Me, sitting atop my car and staring at the windmill, at its sails and at its power. From here, I don't know, I just feel I can handle anything life hands me, that nothing in the world can stop me. I've never shared my bluff with anyone else, not even Janey. Just Annie, and now all of you."

"It's beautiful," Anna said, the others nodding in agreement.

And that's when my emotions took control. I felt a tear coming on, but in front of these three I knew I had to remain strong. So stifling the swell of tears and swallowing the lump that lodged in my throat, I sat there trying to embrace the comfort these friends brought me. But what I most wanted to hear was Janey's vibrant laughter, her infectious charm. I wanted Annie, too, to hear her that voice which would help see me through these next important days in my life. That was my wish, and as I watched the windmill's giant sails turn and turn and turn, I imagined my wish upon the wind, where perhaps, maybe, hopefully, it would be granted.

CHAPTER NINE

The next day was Christmas Eve, and so John and Anna, Rebecca and Junior, all left before noon because they had their own plans and their own holiday to enjoy. In fact, they were all headed for New York, the former duo expected at Anna's family's house for a traditional Italian feast, the latter planning to celebrate the holiday by eating in nice restaurants and taking in a couple of shows. "We don't do traditional Christmases," Rebecca explained, standing before her sleek black BMW.

"Do you do this every year?" Janey asked.

"Since the divorce," Junior replied.

"Five years," Rebecca remarked.

"Then it is a tradition—yours," she instructed them. "That's what Brian taught me."

Janey and Junior had returned to the farmhouse the next morning, joined us all for a big breakfast, the two of them exchanging e-mail addresses afterwards so they could keep in touch. We were getting so technological in Linden Corners, the outside world could not be ignored. But both Rebecca and I were pleased that the two of them had gotten along so well; maybe our distant family had taken a step in the right direction, childhood urging our feet forward.

I hugged Rebecca and told her to, on this solemn day for the Duncan family, "Remember Philip."

"That's why I came to see you in Linden Corners, so we both could."

As we watched both cars pull out of the driveway, Janey waved and then when they were out of sight, she stared up at me and said, "I like Junior," her eyes sparkling like diamonds. I bent down and embraced her.

"You did a very good thing, Janey—I'm proud of you. From all Rebecca has told me about Junior, he doesn't make friends too easily. So it must have been a nice surprise for him to have an instant friendship with you; though it hardly surprises me. Look at you and me, right? We clicked from the very moment we met."

"Junior just needed someone to pay attention to him," she said, a sudden cloud of concern crossing her face. "I need to go back to Cynthia's now, she and I have some last minute holiday details to take care of."

I let her go without another word, mostly because I was afraid my voice might fail me. Janey's enigmatic statement about needing attention reawakened my paranoid feelings, not that they were sleeping too deep down in begin with. What I couldn't be certain was whether I'd been the target for her words. Time and attention to Janey had never been a concern before, something that had never been questioned or been at issue. Given her mood shifts and the unspoken gulf that existed between us, given the fact that today was Christmas Eve and those hidden fears of her could have bubbled to the surface, anything was possible.

My impulse was to run after Janey but in the end I left her alone, for now. Instead, I called Cynthia a half hour later, explained that I was going to run a few errands, "no problem, Brian, Janey's fine here." While I was out I picked up a last minute gift for the children's charity tree at St. Matthew's Church. We were all scheduled to attend the seven o'clock vigil mass, a special celebration for the children of Linden Corners. It was another tradition, Gerta had informed me, saying "George and I took our four daughters every year while they were growing up. How inspiring that mass is, it does such good for our community and others, for the less fortunate." Gerta planned to attend as well, since she explained that one of her four daughters was coming home for Christmas. "She and Dave and the kids will arrive late." As I ran my errands, I found myself looking forward to the mass and being at Janey's side. I was gone for nearly two hours, and then, thinking Cynthia had things to do other than taking care of Janey, I drove directly to her home. Bradley answered the door.

"Hey, Bri, what's up?"

"Oh, I just came to pick up Janey."

"Really? She's not here."

I recalled only one car in the driveway when I pulled up, and so assumed that Cynthia had taken Janey with her.

"Well, Cyn did go out, but not with Janey," Bradley said, running a hand across an unshaven jaw. He was enjoying time off from the law firm through the end of the year. "That's strange, Bri. We told Janey to call you, you know, make sure you were home. She told us you were."

Which meant wherever Janey really was, she was unsupervised and alone. A level of panic I'd never before felt surfaced in me, and I reacted with gut instinct. I raced back to my car, yelling out, "I'll call you when I find her," then peeled out of the driveway just as Cynthia was approaching it. From behind the wheel her eyes widened in surprise, but I kept driving, figuring Bradley could explain what was happening. I hadn't the time. Not a minute passed before I was back at the farmhouse, running inside the house, calling out, "Janey, Janey, are you here?" But there came no reply other than the hollow echo of my own voice. Even though I knew the house was empty, I still did a thorough search from basement to attic and everywhere in between just to be certain. She was nowhere to be found. I stood in her room, feeling absolutely helpless. An idea hit me and I dropped to me knees, poked my head under her bed. The box was gone. Just then the phone rang and I ran to my bedroom, grabbed it on the third ring.

"Janey?"

"I guess that means you didn't find her," I heard Cynthia say.

"No. Cyn, did anything happen while she was over at your house?"

"Nothing that I can think of. All we did was wrap some gifts. She seemed happy."

"Thanks," I said, hanging up without saying good-bye.

I picked the phone back up and dialed the Baker home, hoping Ashley's mother answered. Instead, I heard Ashley herself and when I said who was calling I imagined that horrible little tongue of hers sticking out at me.

"Have you seen Janey?" I asked her.

"No, Brian, she's not here. She's mad at me anyway, so there."

And she hung up on me.

For a moment I wondered why Janey would be mad at her best friend. What was going on? Could Ashley have been jealous of Janey's newfound bond with Junior? Had the girls had a fight, and was that reason behind Janey disappearance? The why could wait, I was more concerned with the basic questions: where was she?

I returned to the kitchen, trying to think of where Janey might have gone off to—on Christmas Eve of all days.

"Janey, where did you go?" I said aloud.

Surrounded by reminders of Annie—her windmill knickknacks that ranged from salt and pepper shakers to coffee mugs and the clock upon the wall—inspiration hit me. I dashed out of the house without my coat, noticing that the snow had begun to fall again, big wet flakes that clung to my sweater. I made my way down the hill to the windmill, hoping I had guessed right. We all have our special places where we can hide from the world, I had shown my friends mine last night, sitting atop Brian's Bluff. For Janey, the windmill was hers because it was where she felt the closest to Annie, where Annie too had felt so safe from her troubles.

The front door was locked. But there was always Annie's emergency key. So I reached down under the tower and grabbed hold of the spare, had the door unlocked in seconds. I flipped on the lights and looked around. Catching no sight of Janey, I called out her name. Again, there came no reply, unless you counted a slight scuffling sound against the floor. Like shoes scraping against wood. She was upstairs in the studio. I took the steps two at a time, and when I reached the second level Janey's lone figure crept out of the shadows. She was pressed against the far wall, as though she were trying to hide, escape from me.

"Hey," I said.

I didn't approach her, keeping my distance by sitting down on the floor near the staircase. Whatever had been eating away at her these past few weeks, it was all going to come out now, that much I was certain. Because it was almost Christmas and because she was Janey and I was Brian and this was supposed to be our first holiday together, it was supposed to be perfect. A special time, and instead it had been spiraling out of control for weeks now.

"You want to tell me what's wrong?"

"Nothing. I'm just visiting Momma."

"Janey, you lied to Cynthia and Bradley. You told them that I was home when you knew very well that I wasn't," I said, the instilled fear in my voice overpowering my firm tone. "Which meant you were here all by yourself. You're still too young for that, sweetie, you know that."

"You can't tell me what to do—you're not my father."

Ooh, I believed we had hit a nerve. This was good, a verbal jab indicating an opening move.

"I know I'm not your father, Janey, never in a million years would I presume that. But I am here to look after you; I'm here because I want to look after you."

"For now," she said.

"For now? What's that supposed to mean? Where is it you think I'm going?"

"Home."

"I am home, Janey—the farmhouse is my home."

"For now," she repeated. "Until you get tired of living here. And then you'll go back to New York and be with your friends. Because that's where you really want to live, you just came to Linden Corners by accident."

"Accidentally, yes, but also on purpose," I said, hoping she would remember this strange dichotomy of words from an earlier discussion. "And I love living here. The life I had in New York, sure I had some fun times. But they weren't always fun. Some days I had to wonder what I was working toward—sure I had a good job and probably would have been very secure money-wise. But would I have been happy? I mean truly happy, fulfilled? Not the way I am here, with you. Janey, your Momma and I didn't ask to fall in love—in fact, we resisted it for as long as we could. Fate had another plan, and so she and I started to think about a future together."

"That's what you always do, Brian, Momma wasn't anyone special to you," she said.

I was taken aback by not only the words but the violent force behind them. As though Janey truly believed such a harsh scenario. What could have given her such a ridiculous idea?

"You wanted to marry that Lucy girl, the one you loved from high school. That's what Rebecca said. And then John told me all about that woman Maddie. You were going to marry her, too, you even bought a ring to give to her. And you never married either one of them, so why would you have married Momma? You could always find another woman to marry—because that's what everyone wants to do, get married. Look at Mark and Sara, maybe John and Anna—they'll probably get married. And so will you, and when you do you'll leave me."

"Oh, my God, Janey," I said, "Oh, no, that's not true, not true at all." She was an emotional wreck. Tears had welled up in my eyes and I tried to wipe them away to no effect, because more quickly showed up until it became a steady stream. Still, I couldn't wallow in my own tears, I needed to find a way to soothe Janey's own wounded feelings. Her lips were trembling and she had retreated into herself, her arms encircled around herself like a cocoon. Emotionally she had closed herself down. Somewhere out there, in my mind or in Annie's spirit or riding the current of the wind existed wondrous words that would open her up again, return to me the infectiously happy Janey Sullivan I'd known. I hoped I could find them.

"Janey, it's true that I had hoped to marry Lucy—but I was very young then and what did I know? My life hadn't really taken shape, I needed to discover where I belonged. So with John's help I moved to New York and eventually I met Maddie. At that time in my life, Maddie and I wanted the same thing and we thought we could find it together. But as you get older, you realize what might have once been important no longer is. What matters is the people in your life, not your achievements. When I left New York, my life changed again, and I found myself looking for that something special. That someone special. Actually, it's beyond special, I wanted someone so great and so wonderful that I'm not even sure there's a word for it. With Annie—your Momma—I thought I had found that person. But really, who I had found was you. Janey, that day at the windmill? I count it as one of the luckiest of my life. It changed my life; you changed my life—for the better, and for always." I paused, trying to collect my thoughts, wondering if this insecurity of hers had led her to hide my ornament; was it really that simple? "Janey, do you know why I took you to my parents' house for Thanksgiving? And why I took you to New York to see the tree?"

"Because you miss your home."

"No, sweetie, I took you there because I wanted to show you who I was before I came to live in Linden Corners," I said. "To share a part of my life with you. That's how you get to know someone, you learn about them."

By this time she was crying and the distance between us be damned, I went running to her and I held her and she held me, her sobs muffled because she was pressing so tight against me. I soothed her soul, I smoothed her hair and kissed the top of her head and I assured her that everything was okay. Still, I searched inside me for one last piece of inspiration, solid proof that could finally settle Janey's fears. Surrounded by Annie's things, her paintings and her easel and her brushes, the very essence of the spirit imbued within her, I realized exactly what I needed to do.

As Janey's tears subsided, I said to her, "Do you remember your Momma talking about a special place of hers?"

She nodded, sniffling at the same time. "Right here, Brian, the windmill."

"Well, yes, that's right. Except I mean before she became known as the woman who loved the windmill. Before she had even met your father."

Janey was thinking hard, I could almost see the wheels turning inside her mind. Suddenly she got up from the floor and wandered over to Annie's drawer full of paintings. Silently she started flipping through them one by one until she came to the particular one she was looking for. Proudly she displayed a beautifully rendered painting, its lush colors as vibrant as Janey herself. It had been drawn from atop a hill, an illustration of the mighty Hudson River and environs, the lovely sky that covered it, the lush green landscape that encased it.

"Momma liked the river, it's where she went to think."

"How would you like to go there now?"

"But Brian, I don't know where it is. Momma never took me. She never took anyone; besides only she could ever find it."

"She took me, Janey, once," I said, "And today—Christmas Eve—I'm going to take you."

Janey's eyes were alive with sudden wonder, brighter now than any collection of lights, even those that adorned the windmill itself. And what did those eyes say to me? That there were discoveries yet to be made, gifts still to come.

* * *

The time was four o'clock and daylight still rode above us. Before long, though, nightfall would settle over the tiny village of Linden Corners. Snow was continuing to float down from the sky, and from what the weather reports indicated it would most assuredly be a white Christmas. In the past hour alone an inch of powder had accumulated on the road, making conditions less than ideal for driving. But I'd assured Janey that she could visit Annie's Bluff—as I had dubbed it this past summer, the precursor to my own Brian's Bluff—and nothing would stop me. Janey and I had bundled up against the cold, and then hopped into the car, one last trip for us before the holiday.

Annie's Bluff was located atop a high hill that provided magnificent vistas of the Hudson River and the surrounding valleys. For some people, this was just one of many views of the river, nothing particularly thrilling. For Annie though, it had held such significance because it was where she had found direction in her own life, the place she'd come to for answers. And a place she had shared only with one other person, me, at a time when neither of us knew what we meant to the other. The time had come to pass this privilege onto the next generation. So I parked the car at the base of the hill, just off the side of the road. Then, I grabbed hold of Janey's mitten-encased hand and guided her up a snowy path. We emerged from a cluster of trees into a snow-covered clearing. Where once sunshine had dappled down on a picnic that Annie and I shared, today only the wind welcomed us, but the wind powered the windmill and the great mill was our friend. Below us lay the grand waters of the Hudson River, icy floes making their way down river, a lone barge trudging through in the wintry storm. We waved to the passing boat, doubting the captain could see us. Then he sounded his horn at us, a foghorn that rippled across the wind. Janey went dashing along the bluff, dancing atop a large rock that grew up from the ground.

"Oh, Brian, it's so pretty up here, that's why Momma loved it so," Janey said, her eyes marveling at the sight before her. "I bet on some nights you can see the moon, practically even touch it. That would be my wish."

"That's a nice wish, Janey. Always remember to send your wishes out upon the wind and know they can come true."

As she gazed up at me, I expected to see a joyful child at my side. Instead I saw the worry return to her face, wrinkles crinkling her freckled nose.

"What's wrong, sweetie?"

"I'm sorry, Brian."

I bent down and hugged her. "That's okay, Janey, you don't have anything to be sorry about. Just remember, whenever anything is troubling you, you have to come and tell me. I made a promise to your Momma that I would always be there for you, when you're happy and when you're sad, when you're sick or when you just want to sit quietly by yourself. Maybe what I need to do is make you that same promise, and there's no better place to do it than here upon Annie's Bluff, with a big open sky before us so your Momma can look down and listen, see the magic that she created."

And that's exactly what I did, amidst the drifting snowflakes and cool night wind, warmth spreading directly from her smile to my heart, winter and its chill having absolutely no effect on us.

* * *

The ride home was less than pleasant. The plows hadn't come by and the roads were icy and slick. It was past six when we returned safely to the farmhouse, just enough time to spare for us to grab a quick meal and get changed before attending the children's vigil mass at St. Matthew's. I sent Janey to put on her prettiest dress of red crushed velvet, while I went to put on a suit. After tying the tie, I knocked on her door and asked if she needed help.

"Maybe with the bow I want to wear in my hair, I'll come down in a moment."

I checked my watch, saw that it was six-forty. "Let's go, let's go."

Back downstairs, I retrieved the gift for the St. Matthew's Christmas tree from under our own tree, and when I turned around there stood Janey. She looked positively aglow in that velvety red dress, which shimmered against the colored lights from the tree. There was only one thing wrong with this picture, her quivering lips. Fear once again stabbed at my heart.

"Hey, what's wrong?" I asked. But standing beside the tree, all lit and glittering with tinsel, I realized what it was. Though we had come a long way today, one issue remained to be dealt with.

"I'm sorry, Brian," Janey said, withdrawing from behind her back the box that had once contained my family Christmas ornament. "So sorry," she repeated and then she broke down into sobs, great heaving sobs that sent her little body shivering. My God, the fear she must have been holding inside her. Forgetting about the box, I took Janey into my arms and held her, comforted her and soothed her, wishing there were instant, magical words that could wipe away the hurt that lay before us.

"Why, Janey, why did you hide it from me?"

She was still weeping but she was trying to talk, too. "I…I didn't, Brian, I didn't even know where it was…not until yesterday. Junior found the box under my bed when we were playing hide and seek in my room. But the box was empty, Brian, I swear. The ornament was gone, but I never took it, honestly. I know it means so much to you, so I had to figure out what did happen to it. It couldn't have just disappeared."

Her words struck deep at my heart, so much so I felt it bleed. All these weeks I'd been consumed with why Janey wouldn't confess to have taken the ornament and now I was faced with the undeniable truth: she was innocent of the crime. She never knew it was gone. My God, how could I have thought Janey would do such a thing? How easily I had assigned blame and then not done anything about it. As I listened to Janey's explanation, a newfound fear gripped at me. She couldn't be so upset for having found just the box, she must have found the ornament as well. Which meant there was another problem—and I wasn't going to like what it was. I opened the lid. And that's when I saw that the beautiful blue glass ball was in pieces, shards as shiny as ever, like thousands of stars dotting the sky.

"Ashley took it, Brian. That first day I showed it to her, I told her I was jealous that you had such a pretty ornament and I didn't. When I told her everyone in your family had one, she said that just meant I wasn't part of your family. So she took it, she was just trying to be my friend. When Junior found the empty box, I knew Ashley had to have the ornament. And I also knew I had to get it back, so I went running off from Cynthia's and went to Ashley's house and took it back. That's why I was gone earlier. On the way home, Brian, oh, Brian, I dropped it."

And she began to cry again. Quickly I set the box down and I took Janey into my arms once more, trying to assuage her fears and her guilt. How horrible she must have felt. "Oh, Janey, it's just a trinket, something to put on the tree. Just...just something from my past. You, though, you're what matters, okay, sweetie? Sure, I'm upset that it's broken, but I don't blame you, how could I?

"Brian, will you tell me about the ornament sometime? Junior told me a little about your brother, Philip, but I don't know what he has to do with your ornament. I want to know about your Christmases past, about your traditions. Will you tell me about Philip?"

I nodded, wiping away my own tears. "Sure," I said, "When the time is right. Right now, we've got to get to church, okay?"

She nodded.

"Brian, are you mad at me?"

"No, Janey, I could never be mad at you," I said, deciding we'd had enough emotional strife for one day. "I'm sorry for all that's happened, Janey, between us. Can we call it even, start fresh?"

"So you're not going anywhere?"

"Janey, I'm right where I belong."

She nodded. "And I'm right where I belong, too."

"There's no other place, sweetie."

I affixed the red bow to her hair and when I pronounced her perfect, "Absolutely perfect," she giggled, and I felt like she was once again the Janey who had saved my life.

"Come on, then, we can't be late for Christmas, right?"

"Yeah," she said.

I didn't correct her this time.

As we headed back out into the snow, I found myself smiling. Because there were still some surprises left in this holiday.

CHAPTER TEN

According to the wooden sign posted at the village limits, the population of Linden Corners was 724 people and give or take a couple dozen, it seemed as through everyone had turned out to celebrate Christmas with their families and with each other, a testament to the sense of community that I had felt from the very moment I stepped into its environs. Of course folks from some of our neighboring towns came as well, the St. Matthew's Children's Christmas Pageant was infamous in these parts. St. Matthew's sanctuary was decorated with three trees that towered to the ceiling, all of them alight with sparkling white lights, their gleam caught in the flickering candles that stood atop the altar. A manger scene was set before the altar, the baby Jesus not yet resting in his cradle. And all around us, the smell of incense and the scent of pine reminded us all that Christmas was upon us. Gerta sat at my side and Cynthia and Bradley were in the row behind us and lots of other familiar faces filled the pews, parents who waited with anticipation for the start of the mass.

The choir began to sing "O Come All Ye Faithful," the triumphant blast of an accompanying trumpet raising the roof on our celebration. Then began the procession with a trio of altar boys, the lead carrying a large brass cross, the other two with long, burning candles. Behind them followed a cherubic young boy, carrying in his hands the baby Jesus who would be placed in the manger. Next came four adults who would say the readings and help with communion and at last was the parade of children, thirty of them dressed brightly for the holiday, the girls with red bows in their hair and the boys with green ties set against crisp white shirts. Bringing up the end of the procession was Father Eldreth Burton, the pastor of our little church. As the music swelled and the sound enveloped the church, the lead child placed the baby Jesus in the manger and the other children placed their gifts beneath the trees until the sanctuary was overfilled with an abundance of giving.

I had caught a glimpse of Janey, herself part of the children's parade. With her colorfully-wrapped present and her face lit with glee, she was like a vision. I watched with unwavering pride, imagining how the other parents felt, knowing they shared with their children a larger bond, a blood connection. Still, Gerta squeezed my hand and remarked to me how wonderful Janey looked, "so healthy and filled with love. And we all know who to thank for that."

"All of us," I said quietly.

The children rejoined their families in the pews, and as Janey sat down between us I told her what a great job she had done. The mass then continued, prayers were spoken and Father Burton delivered a short sermon about the real truth of Christmas and how the best gifts weren't beneath any tree. I knew mine, the sweet little girl who sat between me and Gerta.

As communion ended, Father Burton returned to his seat and like magic, the lights throughout the church were dimmed. The gentle sound of a piano could be heard and moments later, the tender voice of a man's dulcet baritone. Not another sound could be heard throughout the church as the man sang a hymn called "Joseph's Song," a remarkable and powerful song whose lyrics spoke volumes to me, the words, "Not of my flesh, but of my heart," seemingly directed at me and Janey. The song came to an end and the congregation sat still in utter and absolute silence. All around us was the power of Christmas, its message becoming more clear to me on this occasion than any I could ever recall. The lights came back, and the mass concluded.

Afterwards, I shook the singer's hand and thanked him profusely for his heartfelt song.

"I liked it, too," Janey said.

As the church emptied with Father Burton shaking hands with the departing parishioners, I asked Gerta to wait beside Janey. I needed a moment alone. I went against the tide of the crowd, making my way forward to the sanctuary, where I kneeled before the manger. Glancing at the ceramic figurines of Mary and Joseph, at parents who had never asked to be but knew in their hearts that destiny had chosen them, I felt a sudden kinship with them. That's when I laid down one last gift, setting it inside the manger for safe keeping.

Janey and Gerta were waiting at the back of the church.

"You okay, Brian?" Gerta asked.

"Yeah, I'm great."

"Don't say 'yeah'," Janey instructed me, and even though the solemnity of the evening vigil still pervaded, I laughed aloud. My voice carried throughout the church, more so when we stepped outside, the wind billowing past and catching it.

We wished Gerta a wonderful Christmas with her daughter Nora and family, and then Janey and I returned to the car and headed back to the farmhouse, the still-falling snow dancing in my headlights. Nearly a foot of snow had dropped already, and it showed no sign of stopping, not on this cold, blustery Christmas Eve night.

I got Janey to sleep by eleven, just after she had placed a few wrapped packages beneath the tree, telling me "don't peek." I considered reading to her 'Twas the Night Before Christmas, "just like Momma used to do," but then decided upon another story.

"What's the story?"

"The story of the greatest gift of all," I said, settling onto her bed. "Once upon a time, the most special person lived. His name was Philip and he decided one year that he wanted to give the best presents of anyone in his family, and so that's what he set out to do. He found these beautiful glass ornaments—red and blue, green and gold—and had one made for each person in his family. 'Put their names on it, I like that touch,' he told the glass blower, who had in his workshop silver glitter, the color of tinsel. And so that's what happened, one Christmas morning the family awakened and under the tree were these pretty packages—just like the ones you placed downstairs—and the family opened them. There was a glistening red ball with the name Kevin on it, and a green one that read Didi, and then the gold one that said Rebecca and the blue one that read Brian. They came with a note, each of them."

"What did the note say?"

"It said to remember him always—at each Christmas—and to always remember that Christmas means happiness and it brings families together. That's what he taught the family, Janey, and each year they remember his lesson when they place the ornaments on their tree. Ever since then, each of them has tried to live out his legacy—remembering that giving is greater than receiving."

"I like that story," Janey said. "Are you sad, Brian, not to have your name ball?"

"What I've learned just today, Janey, is that I didn't need the ornament to remember Philip. I can honor him in another way, by passing along his story. I call it 'The Greatest Gift'." Then I kissed her good-night. She closed her eyes and I watched as she drifted off to sleep.

Returning to the warmth of the living room, I sat in the recliner and stared at the glistening Christmas tree, knowing I needed to brave the outdoors and retrieve all of Janey's presents from inside the windmill. I felt a yawn overcome me. I was exhausted from the activity of the past few days, the planning and execution of the tavern party and the emotional catharsis Janey and I had gone through earlier today. I was spent and so I closed my eyes for the briefest of moments, thinking about the end of the story I hadn't told Janey, of discovering my brother

Philip asleep in his bed that Christmas morning. But he hadn't been sleeping and he would never again awaken. Philip Duncan had been twenty-three years old; I'd been eleven.

And beneath the tree, there had been no "Philip" ornament.

* * *

"Brian, Santa didn't come, look, there's no presents!"

I jumped up from the recliner, surprised at not only Janey's voice but at the words spewing from her tiny mouth. Rubbing my eyes, trying to rid myself of the sleep demons that still clung to me, it dawned on me that morning had arrived. Christmas morning.

"Of course he did, Janey, he must have..." When I looked down at the near-empty floor beneath the tree my mouth closed. All that waited beneath the tree were the gifts Janey had set out last night. Words failed me.

And I had failed Janey. For over a month my only concern had been giving Janey the most perfect Christmas ever and here it had arrived and what had I done but fallen asleep before being able to set out the gifts. But they were nearby and that's what I told Janey, "They're in the windmill, all the gifts."

"That's where you're supposed to hide them, Brian—but on Christmas morning, they're supposed to be under the tree."

Inspiration struck me as I suggested we go and retrieve them together. Janey liked that idea, it was the windmill after all, and so she ran up and dressed in her warmest clothes and so did I. As we stepped out onto the back porch, we saw that the snow had stopped and that sunshine was brightening the white blanket of snow that covered the land.

"Wow, that's a lot of snow, Brian. How do we get to the windmill now?"

"Easy," I said, and went trudging through deep piles of snow, some drifts higher than others because of the wind that had blown over the open field. I made my way to the barn and inside grabbed hold of the red toboggan. I returned to the back porch and asked Janey to hop aboard.

"Not yet," she said.

Then she ran back inside the house, only to return with an armful of gifts.

"We can open them all in the windmill, Brian, that way Momma can see. She can have Christmas with us."

So maybe falling asleep last night had been the perfect thing, because what we ended up with was the perfect Christmas setting. Janey hopped aboard the toboggan, setting the gifts in front of her and then I took hold of the string and began to make my way through the snow. Once we reached the hill, I set Janey off, the sled racing downward with exponential speed, her gleeful laughter filling the air. I did my best to chase after her, but the drifts were too big and too difficult to maneuver and more than once I fell forward. By the time we arrived at the windmill, I was nearly covered in snow.

"You look like a snowman," Janey said.

"Oh yeah, how'd you like to be a snowgirl," I said, and then with a devilish grin crossing my face I pushed her backward into a large drift. A puff of white powder flew into the air as she hit the ground, downy flakes drifting down on her face. "See, a snowgirl."

Janey began to move her arms and legs back and forth and in moments she had gone from a girl to an angel.

"Look, Brian, I'm making a snow angel."

"Oh, yeah, I'll make a bigger one," and I tossed myself down in the snow and began jerking back and forth, wondering what John might think of me at this moment. He'd think the farm boy had finally cracked his eggs. Janey informed me that I was just making a mess and when I got up and looked at my handiwork, I had to admit she was right. Her angel looked so perfect and mine, well, like an angel having a seizure. I suggested we open some gifts instead, only to find the entrance to the windmill was blocked by even more snow. Not even the spare key would help us now.

"This isn't the easiest Christmas I've ever had," Janey said.

"But it sure is fun, isn't it?"

I looked around at our surroundings, searching for a solution to our dilemma. Once last summer in a moment of desperation I had reached the second level of the windmill by climbing the sails, but today they were turning, and even though their rotation was gentle I didn't want to risk injury. So I returned to the barn, again going slowly, delaying our morning celebration even more. But when I made my way back, I carried with me a ladder. I set it against the rear of the windmill, climbed to the catwalk with the gifts in my hand. Then Janey began her ascent and I grabbed hold of her while she maneuvered her way under the railing. A knight returning his princess to the tower after a grand adventure. From there I opened the access door and we entered directly into Annie's studio on the second floor.

I turned on a light but we both left on our coats, since the cold had permeated through the wooden walls of the mill. Remembering that I had stored a couple blankets inside the mill, just as Annie had done, I retrieved one of them and set it on the floor. Janey sat down on the blanket, where I proceeded to place before her piles of gifts wrapped in shiny paper that showed reindeer and Santa and snowmen.

I sat beside her and watched as she began unwrapping each gift. Janey was a typical little girl in her likes, dolls in which you could play dress up and so there was a new Barbie and several different designer outfits for the doll; there were some clothes too for Janey, and several stuffed animals, friends for her favored purple frog. Finally there remained just two more gifts, and I presented the first one to her with excitement.

"This is from your past," I said.

"What is it?" she asked.

"Unwrap it and find out."

She began to tear at the paper. Underneath she revealed one of Annie's paintings, newly framed and protected by a glass covering. I had gone back and forth on which painting would be perfect, thinking maybe the one of Annie's Bluff, thinking maybe one of the windmill pictures. In the end, I settled upon the painting of a very young Janey cradled in the arms of Dan and Annie Sullivan, the two of them proud new parents.

"Thanks, Brian, I love this gift so much. It helps me remember, especially my father."

"We'll hang it in your room, okay?"

"That's the perfect place," she said, hugging me so tight I thought I might explode with emotion.

"There's one more gift, Janey."

"But you've already given me too much," she said.

Seeing her surrounded by the numerous gifts, perhaps she was right. I had spoiled her, but if ever a little girl deserved to be spoiled, well, here she was. So that's when I handed her the last gift. "This gift is from your future."

She gazed up at me with wide eyes, then returned them to the small, square box. Gently she unwrapped the present, opening the box she discovered beneath the bright paper. As she discovered what lay inside that box, her mouth dropped with wonder and surprise.

"Oh, Brian..."

"Go ahead, take it out of the box."

And she did, and what she saw was her very own Christmas ornament, a shiny red glass ball, the name "Janey" lettered in silver glitter.

"Consider that one a gift from Uncle Philip," I said. "Just as I'm part of your family, you are now irretrievably part of mine. And nothing can ever change that, not anymore."

Janey had no words in her little frame. Lucky me, I had to settle for a hug, one that lingered for minutes, until I could feel her sweet tears seeping through my shirt.

"You're welcome," was all I said.

Finally, she returned the ornament to the box. Then she informed me that I had to open up my gifts. There were two boxes, the first of which contained a 3-D jigsaw puzzle called "The Spectacular Spinning Dutch Windmill," which Janey informed me "really spins." I told her what a special gift it was, how I looked forward to the two of us building the windmill, "Something we seem to be very good at." The second gift was a box of staples—"You know, for the staple gun." You used up an awful lot when you decorated the windmill with all those lights." I laughed at this second gift, treasuring the sentiment behind it.

"But those are just fun gifts, Brian. I wanted to get you something really special and I asked Gerta and Cynthia and even John, when he showed up for the party. They all kept telling me you already had the gift you wanted."

"You," I said.

"Hey, that's what they said. But Brian, that wasn't enough, not for me. So the decision was mine—to find the best gift in the whole wide world. So I got you something I think we'll both like." From the inside of her jacket she pulled out an envelope and handed it to me. "It's the other reason I disappeared yesterday from Cynthia's. I went to town all by myself—I know I'm not supposed to but I just had to, Brian, I had to get this card from Marla's store. I knew she carried lots of cards.

It was on my way home from Ashley's." She paused, momentarily looking away from me. "That's when I dropped the ornament, Brian, when I was buying the card."

I looked at Janey with surprise, at her ingenuity and at her boldness, her impulsiveness and at the tragic irony too, of her tale. She must have been very determined to get me this particular gift to have risked so much. So without further ado I opened the back flap of the envelope and withdrew the card. As soon as I saw the writing on the front, my lips quivered and a wave of emotion rippled up and down my spine; my eyes blurred with tears and I almost couldn't read the words. But I could never forget them though, because what it said was, "For My Dad, At Christmas." On the inside of the card she had written, "To my new Dad, Merry Christmas, Love, Janey." I was left without a single word on my tongue.

"I'm only eight and I have lots of growing to do and I'm going to need help," she said. "After I bought the card I came immediately to the windmill because I needed to ask Momma if it was all right that I have a new Dad. She's my Momma and she always will be and my father will always be my father. But you can have a Dad, too, that's what I learned—Junior taught me that."

"Janey, you bought this card yesterday? Before we talked? But...you were so worried that I might want to return to my old life and get married. You thought..."

"Yes, Brian, that's what I thought. That's what my head was telling me. My heart, though, it knew what to feel. So, will you, Brian, will you be my new Dad?"

"I think I already am," I said.

With a squeal that echoed far and wide, Janey jumped into my arms and I didn't let her go, not for the longest time, relishing this moment with the little girl who on this most giving of holidays had given the best gift of all, her unconditional love, her heart. I couldn't believe this incredible gesture, this most wondrous and unimaginable sacrifice.

"Come on," I finally said, "Let's go hang your new Christmas ornament on the tree."

When we returned to the farmhouse and came to the shiny tree, Janey and I held the ornament and together found just the perfect branch for it.

* * *

The phone rang around noon. Janey was playing with her new toys and I was still marveling over the card she had given me. I would treasure it forever, just as I would

Janey herself. When I picked up the receiver, I heard Gerta say, "Merry Christmas, Brian." I returned the greeting and asked how her holiday morning had gone.

"Fine, just fine," she said, though her voice lacked conviction.

"Gerta, who's there with you?"

"Oh, I'm fine, Brian, just fine."

"Gerta?"

That was the second time she'd said those words, and they sounded rehearsed and hollow. As I recalled the constant snowfall of the night before, a sneaking suspicion crept upon me.

"Gerta, your daughter couldn't make it, could she? The snow stranded her at her home, didn't it?"

"I told her not to attempt it, the roads were horrendous. They still are."

"So you're alone?"

"I'm fine, Brian..."

"Yeah, I didn't believe you the first two times you said it. Hang on, Gerta, it's Janey and Brian to the rescue."

"No...Brian, really the roads—don't chance it."

"I won't," I said.

"What are you plotting, Brian Duncan?"

"Oh, nothing much, but I might be just passing through," I said, replacing the receiver. I called out to Janey that we had a special errand to run. Once again we bundled ourselves against the winter cold, once again we loaded a few presents into the sled and Janey took up her position at the back of the red toboggan. I took hold of the string and then we were off.

The back roads hadn't been plowed; everyone was taking a holiday today. But that meant there were no cars on the road, giving me and Janey and the red sled free reign. It was a two-mile trek to the Connors' home and we spent the time it took to get us there by singing Christmas carols, ending with "Frosty the Snowman" as we headed up Gerta's driveway. As we reached her porch, she emerged from the inside, a smile brightening her face.

"Oh, the two of you get inside right now, it's freezing out there," she said, obviously delighted to see us. "Goodness, what am I going to do with you?"

"Hot chocolate sounds like a good idea," I said.

"With tiny marshmallows," Janey added.

"Absolutely, with tiny marshmallows," Gerta said with a great smile.

The Christmas tree lights were on and music poured out of speakers and from the mantle hung two stockings, one for herself and one in memory of George. I felt a lump lodge in my throat as I thought of Gerta awakening this morning, her first Christmas without George. We hugged her, and then Gerta told Janey that a gift with her name waited for her under the tree.

"Wow, more Christmas presents," Janey said, running to see what gift Gerta had gotten her. As it turned out, more Barbie accouterments. Gerta and I had actually coordinated this.

We settled into the living room and I lit some logs in the fireplace, where before long a burning fire crackled and pine-scented warmth began to envelop us. I passed Gerta her gifts, the first one more or less something to make her smile.

"New pie plates, why Brian Duncan, whatever does this mean?" she asked, laughter in her voice.

"It means he likes your pies, Gerta," Janey said.

The second was another of Annie's paintings, this one representing a scene of the village of Linden Corners in winter, the sign "Connors' Corners" in the background. Like Janey's gift, I had this one framed as well.

"Oh, Brian, what a remarkable idea."

"It's from Janey, too, she's the one who suggested it."

"Momma liked to paint," she explained.

"It's beautiful," she said. "I can almost picture George inside this world."

Gerta informed me then it was my turn to open my gift. It looked like a shirt box but judging from Gerta's expression I believed she was trying to fake me out. Indeed, that proved to be the truth. There was no shirt inside the cardboard, just a folded piece of paper. I unfolded it and began to read. My eyes widened with surprise. I gazed at Gerta and said, "Oh no, I couldn't possibly accept..."

"You will accept it, Brian, no debate."

What I held in my hands was a piece of the past. It was the property deed for the tavern—for the entire building, actually. I wasn't just a bartender, I was the owner of the bar and Mark Ravens's new landlord.

"Gerta, thank you—I don't know what to say. Your generosity..."

"Is unmatched by yours, Brian," she said, laughing. "My goodness, who else would pull a sled for two miles through two feet of snow just to make sure some old lady had company for Christmas. You did that without thinking and that, Brian, is what makes you so special. Janey knows it, and so do I."

"This Christmas, it's been such a rewarding day already," I said. "I feel so rich."

"So does St. Matthew's," Gerta said.

"What do you mean?" I asked, surprised at the turn in the conversation.

"Oh I think you know exactly what I mean, Brian Duncan Just Passing Through," Gerta said. "St. Matthew's received the most extraordinary Christmas gift last evening—after the vigil mass. Father Burton was retrieving the baby Jesus figurine for Midnight Mass when he discovered an envelope had been placed in the manger. An anonymous person had left a cashier's check for twelve thousand, five hundred dollars. A note was attached, asking that the money be used to help those less fortunate."

"Wow," I said.

"Wow is right," Janey said. "That's a lot of money."

That's when I showed Gerta my Christmas present from Janey, the beautiful card. "Some of us received gifts that are priceless. Right, Janey?"

"Right, Dad."

A few minutes later, Janey went to set the table for our Christmas meal and Gerta came and sat beside me, her voice soft.

"Your father gave you a check for twenty-five thousand, Brian. Can I assume you kept the other half?"

I shook my head. "I just couldn't, it didn't feel right," I said. "I donated it to something my parents will hardly object to, though. I sent the other check to the Philip Duncan Cancer Fund."

The snow returned that afternoon, and Janey and I remained at Gerta's, where she cooked the most delicious glazed ham dinner and for dessert, rather than strawberry she went with a peach pie. Surrounded by the two women who had most changed my life, the ever-sweet Gerta and the irrepressible Janey, my first Linden Corners Christmas came to a close. For weeks I had struggled in my search for guidance, from the windmill and from Annie and I guess that wish I had made upon the wind had been heard, because from tragedy had come such goodness, from the people who made my life so full and so rich, so complete.

Two families had shared their Christmas traditions with each other, and in doing so had forged new ones. Maybe not just new traditions were born, but a new family, too, one that went beyond blood, one that was sealed with a powerful thing called love.

I had to wonder if somewhere along the wind's travels Annie had maybe met my brother, Philip.

EPILOGUE

Theirs was a seemingly unbreakable bond, one that had been built by the power of the wind and by the presence of the mighty windmill, which today spun its special brand of magic, even as the uncertainty of a new year presented itself. On this night in December, the last one of the year, he found himself walking through the deep drifts of snow, venturing to the base of the windmill. It was here, on this eve of resolutions, he sought inspiration and knowledge and strength, all of which he would need to negotiate his way through the memories of a past that threatened to undo their fragile happiness. Because as wonderful as they were together, life hadn't always been easy, it came with daily challenges. But the coming year would prove that the two of them could get through anything.

"Annie, can you hear me" he asked aloud, hoping the wind would once again carry his words forward, upward. This time he knew they would. "I wanted to thank you, Annie. Christmas has come and gone. We missed you—

Janey did, I know that, because with everything we planned and everything that we did, always Janey would mention you and tell me about your traditions. I missed you, too, so much. You changed my life, first by entering it and second by leaving it, but in the process you left behind the most wonderful gift ever, the gift of the future. Tomorrow a new year begins—we'll never forget the past and never forget you. The painting of you and Dan and Janey when she was child, it hangs in her room and will forever and always. I think though we'll be able to move forward. We're still getting to know each other, and this past month we had our greatest challenge. When I last spoke to you, I wondered if I was enough for Janey. I think you answered that pretty well for me, for her. What do you think?"

There was no answer, not today. Snowflakes fell lightly, the wind was gentle and the sails spun slowly, as though the windmill itself could anticipate the quiet soon to descend on the tiny village of Linden Corners, on its residents and on its way of life. For Brian Duncan, this new year would be one of wonder, of new experiences. But that's what this past year had been about, that and how he had grown from it. He had little doubt the growing would continue, Janey would continue to teach him. So January was around the corner, the turning of the calendar and the beginning of new chances.

"Annie, I took Janey to meet my parents. She met my sister and my nephew and she even met John, whom you never met and I always wished you had. He's a good guy, even if he still thinks I've become a farmer. But my family, we never talked much about them, mostly because I didn't talk about them. With Janey, though, she's opened up new possibilities for me. Just yesterday my parents called and said they would like to visit, perhaps this spring. Another new awakening for us all. I'll show them the windmill and hopefully they'll begin to understand the choices I've made."

There was another snowstorm headed for Linden Corners, for the entire Hudson River Valley region actually, and for a moment he imagined Annie's Bluff covered with snow, hidden from the world, to be discovered only by himself and Janey, and always together. Just then the wind picked up and the sails began to turn faster.

"You know, Annie, sometimes you're very quiet. Like the woman I met this summer. And sometimes—like now—you make yourself known. Is there something on your mind?"

From the corner of his eye he saw Janey emerge over the hill. With her boots on, she slowly made her way down.

"Oh, I see, you're saying hello. Come to wish your daughter a Happy New Year? That's what we all wish for, Annie, the happiest of them all. I think Janey and I, we're on the road to having one, but know we're never far away. Call to us anytime. Oh, and if you meet a guy named Philip

on your travels, tell him 'The Greatest Gift' lives on, that he lives on."

And the wind whipped past him again, the sails spinning faster before they were once again silenced.

"Come on, Brian, it's almost midnight."

So it was. He had lost track of time. Back at the farmhouse, his guests waited for him. He'd made an executive decision to close the tavern for the night and so Cynthia and Bradley, Mark and Sara, Gerta too, they were all gathered in anticipation of the arrival of a new year.

"Let's not go back, not yet," he said.

Janey stayed at his side, right where she belonged. Minutes later, the clock ticked past midnight and the year of the windmill ended. A new year had begun, its story not yet written, its fate yet to be discovered. In the magical, wind-fueled place like Linden Corners, there were always new stories to tell and new discoveries to be made.

Printed in the United States
130196LV00001B/19-21/P

9 780595 535200